Circle Inn a Circle

A Novel

By

Maria Habershon

The law locks up the man or woman who steals the goose from the common

but lets the greater villain loose, who steals the common from the goose. (c17)

All characters in this book are fictitious, and any resemblance to any persons, living or dead, is purely coincidental.

ISBN 978-1-9164525-0-3

For Phoebe

With heartfelt thanks to my parents, Emma Boston, Susan Hester, Mirella Paganuzzi, and Cathy Jeffrey.

Chapter One

These Eyes

It took some time before I realised that I had been here before. That day, I had taken a different route for my walk and found myself standing next to a village green, encircled within a pole and pillar fence. I somehow remembered the cool sensation of its metal behind my knees. Whilst realising that I had felt this many years before, when swinging myself upside down, a nineteen seventies hit, 'Knock Three Times', began to play in my head. Turning to face the narrow road, the view my much younger self would have seen gradually made sense. The Norfolk knapped flint stone wall, the big house, gatehouse, and The Inn on the Green all spread out before me, as I was bombarded by forgotten images, and emotions; the main one being fear at what now looked like an idyllic place. This Inn had been my home.

****

I recalled our abrupt departure, shortly before my seventh birthday. Sitting in the saloon bar, with my mother and one her friends, whilst awaiting the removal lorry, I inspected the leaving present of a stick of blue eye-shadow; trying to ignore the fact that they were both crying.

Parents do not tell six-year-olds everything in my experience, but as this is about the age when we begin to store memories, I very quickly remembered quite a lot but wanted more information. At once, deciding that they might be more willing to tell their now fifty-something daughter the true history of our time here, I took out my mobile and rang them; my heart thumping in my ears as I waited for someone to connect at the other end.

"Hello, you'll never believe where I am; I'm standing opposite The Inn on the Green." I blurted out, not knowing which of them had lifted the handset.

There was a silence before my mother eventually spoke. "Good grief! That is a surprise. I knew you were in Norfolk but had no idea you were there."

"Neither did I, as I'm not actually staying in the village; I've only now recognised where I am and was just wondering if you could tell me why we left."

I knew this was a lot to throw at an older person and could feel her memory rebooting its self.

"It was very sad," she said, before pausing for what felt like a long time. "There was a death, and people were too much in each other's pockets. We were uncomfortable with it all and knew it was time to move on." From the sound of her voice, I could tell how uneasy she still felt about this. "We were only ever passing through; always meaning to come to London eventually."

I didn't want to upset her and knew it was too much to ask for details, we had moved away, and on with our lives. However curious I felt, it seemed kinder to let the usual conversation play itself out, before I could call off satisfied that I had not stirred up unpleasant memories. I did this but felt guilty in the knowledge that I had brought the subject of The Inn up again.

I'd come away to reboot myself, actually, but had no idea it would be to this extent. Lacking in funds, and the mental focus to scour the internet, I had taken a chalet on a camp site for a few weeks, the first that I came upon; very much intent on being alone. I wondered if I hadn't subconsciously chosen to return here, at what was a difficult time. The alternatives to this being that my arrival here was pure chance or that I had been guided by the insidious hand of the computer world; linking up previous searches I might have made.

However, it did seem that by trying to escape a current anxiety I had, inadvertently, conjured up old ones. Too wrapped up in the present, I had somehow forgotten that I was once someone else, who had existed in another place and time. With these thoughts, I then saw myself, as I had been:

I wore a brown, corduroy dungaree-styled dress, with a little witch-like figure embroidered on the chest pocket; I used to keep stuff in there. I often walked up the few stone steps leading to a grand door, and into the huge Georgian mansion house behind The Inn. Yet, I could not remember if my mother or brother were always with me, when I used to visit. I would climb up a rounding staircase to reach a room which overlooked the car park, and the village.

The resident, I recalled, was an elderly lady in a wheel chair. She would feed me chocolate gingers, which I liked very much, and are still my favourite confection. We would chat whilst she and I watered the plants, arranged on long tables in the huge room.

From the road, looking at the big house, I began to picture other rooms in there; corridors and floors of them. I couldn't imagine why anyone would need so many. These had been mostly empty, apart from the odd chair. I often had dreams of endless rooms and wondered if they stemmed from this time. Looking again at the big house, I was still staggered at the size of the place, in this setting; finding it difficult to imagine that it could just have been a family dwelling.

Avoiding my former home at The Inn, for the present, I stuck to the pavement; passing the gatehouse - hardly daring to give it a glance. Making my way instead across the newish tarmac, towards the big house, I could remember the impressive gravel car park that had once been there – recalling how it used to sound when I was much closer to its then gritty surface. It was a walk you could not make in stealth; your own feet announced their approach. On a hot summer's day, the cool of the earth beneath could almost be felt.

Looking up, I considered how a structure like the grand house before me would be impossibly expensive, and unthinkable, in today's glass and steel world. The eight-windowed frontage was something I had never forgotten but strolling nervously along the side of the building I was shocked at its depth, having somehow lost the fact that it stretched back much further than it was wide; a seemingly endless mass of red brick, with many windows, and a walled court-yard.

The land behind had been filled with caravans, when I was a child, but was now over taken by mock-period barn apartments. I noticed, fixed to a post, planning application for something similar to be made of the house itself. This warren of rooms and corridors was to be chopped, and transformed into apartments. I sank at the idea of the proposed changes; which was stupid really, as it was vastly under-used even forty odd years ago. I would be happy to live there, I thought, with a slight shudder.

Looking around, I remembered there was something about those caravans that used to stand behind the house; I could not quite put my finger on it. We often played around there, my brother and I. I wished that he would remember stuff, but he just cannot, or will not; he lives in the present and marches through it much better than I do. If I had called him, to share in this moment, it would have meant nothing to him.

After studying the house, and the views, for some time, I headed round to The Inn; stopping briefly, as I passed the gate to the small garden of the pub's tenant's. It wasn't a particularly warm day, but I could still smell those summers, and see my child-self digging around in the flower beds for beloved toys that my delightful brother claimed to have buried there; I always fell for it and got in trouble for up-ending plants. Tracing the windows upstairs and down, with new eyes, trying desperately to recall the interior, I noticed some stones missing from its walls. This seemed significant. And then, the beer garden, with its cheerful umbrella covered tables and benches; although large, seemed smaller than it had appeared to me in my memories.

Young women in hotpants paraded across the lawn, pursued by Bobby, the family dog; in search of any concealed chicken. This was a very brief vision, vanished as quickly as it surfaced. As this disappeared from my mind the gatehouse came back into view. It was rented out to holiday makers, back then. I knew I went in there between visitors, when it was being cleaned; feeling certain that we didn't hang around, for some reason. All I could remember was a small flight of stairs, with a child gate at the top.

Having taken in the lie of the land, I entered the pub itself; stepping through a time zone of sorts. The past and present collided, leaving me quite dizzy. This could have been due to the stress I was under, but it felt more that my brain was in over-drive; trying to collate old information. Long unanswered questions attempted to resolve themselves, but there was one that was always lost to me. It was a lovely place, and I couldn't understand the terror it released in me. The smell of ale, that hoppy odour of home, to anyone who has ever lived in a pub, or enjoyed one, led me tentatively to the bar. I switched my brain to the now and enjoyed perusing the possibilities on offer. The elegant pumps suggested a froth of malty indulgence, from behind that familiar polished bar; with its cosy flannel cloths and beer mats. I made my selection, not too strong, just suitable for a lunchtime sup, and found a table in the corner of the empty saloon bar.

In truth, I had enjoyed my time here as a child; I loved it. I had always found it fascinating, and still did. For years after, when visiting our grandparents' house, and believed by all to be asleep, my brother and I would sneak down the stairs, listening from behind the sitting room door; hoping for tales of more, or the same, of when we lived in that pub by the sea.

These are some of the mysteries which came to mind: the dip that would occur at the end of my parents' bed; the dog barking at nothing; my little sleep-walking excursions; the religious statues that lost their heads - we were Catholics; those missing stones; what the hell happened at that hotpants competition and, I was sure, if I thought hard enough about this, many more.

Present anxieties were too tedious, they could bugger off. I chose instead to find myself in a journey though the past. It's not always where you're going that's most important; on occasions, it's where you have been.

Wishing for the power to look back, and, raising my eyes for inspiration, I then saw the beamed ceiling. Its plaster work was far from perfect, despite a recent paint-job I could still discern the old, nicotine-stained edges, and the occasional hole; now, these did attract my attention. We were spies, my brother and I. I began to remember something more; another side to the story of when we were here.

Chapter Two
Shangri-la

I walked back to the campsite with new purpose. In every step I tried to find something lost. I knew I had seen these sights before and sought memories through their details. Yet, passing the houses, and little landmarks, that must have meant something to me back then, I could only recall those holes in the plaster, and blushed inwardly; I had never underestimated children, and was again sure of why I did not.

On reaching the gates, I noticed that my hunger wasn't only for clues; I had forgotten to buy food, and this was a small disaster. Apart from being a necessity to survival, I always look forward to my next meal with relish, despite outwardly being a bit of a stick. I was, therefore, presented with little choice but to dine at the camp clubhouse; I feared the frozen burger and nugget options, as were likely to be on offer in such an establishment. Although, on entering the hut, I was pleasantly surprised that the menu also suggested crab sandwiches, and falafel salads. Another flash back came, this time it was crabs in a washing-up bowl, on the floor in my dad's office. I had completely forgotten that there was even an office at The Inn. Seeing them, resting so peacefully on the scratched surface of that marbled green, rubbery bowl, which had appeared in my head, I settled for the falafel. I dawdled along the tray slide to the till, my mind very much elsewhere, until I came to the cashier.

I, myself, am guilty of dressing in the past, and know that I am probably recognisable at a distance due to my dated clothing. The lady behind the till was known to me in this way. She had a certain style, which she had chosen, or not, to stick with.

It was the double crown that first caught my eye; her head being tipped forward, on reaching for something beneath the counter. At once unmistakable in the way that the hair was naturally shaped around the down turned face; the shoulder length featherings were now gone, but it was a familiar cut none the less. A flash of greying at the roots dissolved into blonde. I knew I had brushed that head, and felt its contours.

As I barely understood what my own place in that time had been, I held back on my usually informal ways; with some effort. I knew that I had known her, but also knew that it would be improbable, without my own announcement, that she would remember me. I was also sure that she must have changed her clothes since nineteen-seventy; one would hope this to be the case for someone working in a food environment, but the t-shirt and fringed suede waistcoat were of the correct era. She was also, somehow, significant.

After paying for my food, giving nothing more than the money, and a thank you, I chose a seat from where I could play detective. It wasn't just her appearance that I recognised; it was her being behind a counter. I felt sure that she had worked at The Inn, behind the bar. I had liked the staff and enjoyed their attention. Apart from when I was at school, or occasionally in the company of family friends, I was usually the youngest child around most of the time. This was hard, I think I was almost irritated by it; I wanted to be older and have some sort of control over things. However, I did recall our being pretty free range.

When your parents run a pub they do not have the time to watch you all day, and unless my memory played tricks on me, I could picture myself, alone, or with my brother, heading to all sorts of destinations in the local area. At other times, I believed, I tagged along with the staff or regulars on little excursions or errands. Was she one of these?

Half the occupants of that village probably did a few shifts at The Inn; during the summer months, at least. That being the nature of a small seaside place, such as this one; much of the work must still be seasonal, I thought.

Again, it was the clothes that triggered something in my memory of life behind the bar; men with farmer's boots, or the oily trousers of a mechanic, pulling pints and collecting glasses.

I picked my way as slowly as I could through the meal, hoping for something to happen; I don't know what on earth I thought would. After watching the diners come and go, I eventually decided on an early night. I tidied my table and made my way to the glass doors. As I was on my way out, I noticed someone else vaguely familiar; a now elderly man in biker's clothes going into a storage building, next to the bungalow within the gates. Apart from those, like my family, who were passing through, I imagined that most players in this story still lived around here. It had now become a sort of story to me, and I had been one of the characters in it; although I had, for the moment at least, lost the plot.

With a strong wind heralding an approaching storm, I was glad to close myself in the little chalet. I could hardly wait to get into bed. Studying my face in the small mirror of the bathroom, as the electric toothbrush rolled its way around my mouth, I looked for traces of the child I had been. There was the chicken pox scar, between my eyes; that had been made here. I remembered sweaty afternoons, stuffed between crumpled sheets, during a hot spring; convalescing in one of the twin beds in my brother's long room. I had my own, with a sloping ceiling and leaded glass windows; I liked it but often preferred to stay with my brother for company, and to avoid being alone when strange things occurred. When the chicken pox cleared, I still couldn't return to school as I had developed a large patch of impetigo, entirely covering my chin. I remembered the crusty scab falling away in my hand, one day in the garden, and fearfully touching my new skin; which to my relief was smooth and soft. I hoped that I didn't put this in my little pocket.

I then let my mind wander around the upstairs accommodation of The Inn, with my head firmly on the pillow which I had bought at no small cost, locally, on arrival; preferring to sleep with my dribble alone. Although things were a bit patchy, I recalled that there were no fitted carpets upstairs; hence our easy access to the floorboards for spying purposes. And then, I considered something else that I often remembered; the secret passage, of sorts, surrounding my brother's old room. This had been created at some point to lessen the drop of the roof, as it was originally a hay loft or attic. We would take turns in making torch-carrying explorations of this, with one of us manning the entrance.

Sometimes, this included bearing strange gifts to leave for the things that went bump in the night.

I remembered, willingly or not, placing the offering of the long, thin box of a Timex watch, that my grandparents had bought me for Christmas, in that dark place. We only had a tiny torch, in the shape of a book; the bulb was no larger than a balled pinhead. I can't imagine how we explained away the state of our knees and socks after those, no doubt, dusty journeys.

We were big Doctor Who fans at the time; my brother, I recalled, had a plastic Dalek. I think my plastic Windy Miller got into some terrible scrapes with this. In real time and space, he was Jon Pertwee's Doctor and I was his able assistant Liz. Everything unusual that went on was played through by us in these roles. We were probably quite brave, when I came to think of it. Things certainly did go bump in the night back then, but I still had a feeling that those were not the things that made me feel uncomfortable at the sight of the place. You cannot expect a building so old to be absent of ghosts, and there certainly were some of those.

Some time before my scabby days, I know I was found sitting at the top of the stairs, in the middle of the night. This was one of the incidents up for discussion at my grandparents' house. Of course, they didn't know the whole story, and nor do I now, but they never even bothered to ask me about it. I was given no opportunity to tell them what I did remember.

Jesus and Mary, relegated to the mantle piece in my room, were travelling to a far off realm in the Tardis, during our play, before going to bed. The mantle piece, also being the deck of the Tardis, they were safely tucked up there when I finally hit the hay and my brother had gone to his room. My mother came up and tucked me in, and I went to sleep, only to be awoken some time later by a tapping on the window. My senses told me that it wasn't from outside, but from within. I kept my eyes firmly shut. Placing all the faith I had in Jesus, Mary, the Doctor and Liz, I fell into the reluctant sleep of a six-year-old. As I said, we were used to bumps in the night. I awoke, with my father standing above me, sitting on the top step, not really knowing how I came to be there, and was ushered into my brother's room and tucked in again.

I woke up before anyone else the next morning and went back into my room. The statues were still on the mantle piece, but their heads were now sitting by their feet. I was confused by this, and never saw them again, nor did I mention them to anyone; apart from my brother.

The events that followed could be related to this incident and a few others, perhaps. Things were murky but becoming a bit clearer.

In my cosy chalet, I fell again into that reluctant sleep, but this time as a fifty-something. Bizarre dreams of the present and past mingled - my brother, looking as he does now, all sensible and suited, making tea in a plastic pot; shushing me, and pointing poignantly to the closed entrance of the secret passage. Those corridors of rooms came yet again, with dusty, ancient chairs; windows looking in and looking out.

There was a huge creak and a crash, and I awoke; the roof had fallen in. It was too dark to see the full extent of the damage, but I felt wood and asphalt, on what had been the empty side of the double bed. Leaves and branches covered me; I pulled myself, feet first, from under their grasp. The meaty taste of my own blood swilled around my mouth, as I crawled about, desperately seeking the door. There was another loud crack as it was pulled open, and to my relief, I saw, from behind my confusion, the familiar figure of the aging biker. I remembered saying "I know you", and then nothing.

I came round slumped forward on the grass; I don't think I was out for more than a moment. "Slow you down there," a man's voice ordered, as I attempted to push myself up. I began to realise that a tree, or at least part of one, had fallen on the chalet, and that I was now in the company of the biker; his boots being firmly planted in my line of vision.

"How're you feelin, young lady? I think you've taken quite a knock there."

I wasn't sure about the young lady, but he was right about the knock; I felt disorientated.

"I'll be fine, thank you," I replied, deciding I would be, however much it hurt to say this; there was some damage to the inside of my right cheek, where I had been bashed by something.

I knew I couldn't stay down there forever, feeling oddly small, and grateful that I was wearing more than my pants, as this wasn't usually the case when I went to bed. The dampness of the ground had begun to gather about the fabric of my baggy, cotton pyjama trousers, and so, again, I made an attempt to get up; this time his hand reached down to help me.

"Come on then, we'd better have a look at you." The leather of the jacket felt surprisingly warm as he placed a capable arm around my shoulders, whilst still holding my hand. My bare feet reinforced a sense of vulnerability, as I was led across the well-tended lawn to the bungalow, at the entrance to the site, where we made our way through the already open door.

"Rachel, I've told him a hundred times to sort that bloody tree out and look at what's happened now."

It was my once feather-haired friend from the clubhouse, wearing a silky, blue kimono style dressing gown. They sat me down and fussed about with salt water, and then a glass of brandy, which I, in vain, tried to refuse.

"Don, you go and make up the spare room while I get…What's your name love?"

"Alice," I was shocked at the sound of my voice, painfully saying my own name, as my sore cheek slapped against my teeth; with this, I had entered it into the play of events.

"While I get Alice here sorted out," she said, giving me a good look over, like she'd only just seen me. They both went off in different directions and left me alone in the sitting room.

There was an open fireplace, a Wurlitzer jukebox, a nineteen sixties Hurdy Gurdy pinball machine, a Chesterfield sofa and an art deco rug; all on a floor of well-varnished oak. In my books, they had done well for themselves.

This was a very cosy place, whether or not they owned it, or the site, but they certainly seemed in charge of it. When I had arrived, three days earlier, a much younger woman had given me the key to my chalet, so I couldn't be sure of their exact position here.

The walls were of a soft pink and covered with many pictures. There were photographs of biking events and family shots, along with prints of local and faraway places. I then came upon something that drew my attention in and out, like the zoom of a camera gone crazy; group photos taken outside The Inn. There was

Bobby, our beloved family dog, leaping through the air in front of a line of people, as the shutter closed its eye.

Before I could take a closer look, Rachel came back, bearing the organised pile of a flannel, a dressing gown, a large towel, toothbrush and toothpaste; immediately followed by Don, who showed me to the guest bedroom.

"There's your own little bathroom, my love. Anything you need, give us a shout."

Again, I found myself studying my own face, this time for new scabs and potential scars. I was relieved that there was nothing much to see, except for a few minor scratches. I rinsed my mouth and took myself to bed, in the strange, lamplit room; still wondering how the hell I came to be there. Tomorrow was going to be an interesting, and awkward, day I was sure. Exhausted, I fell into an unusually, for me, dreamless sleep.

Chapter Three
White Rabbit

I was awoken by the sound of distant buzzing. Looking at the clock on the bed-side table, I was surprised to see that it was half past ten. With some effort, and feeling very stiff, I rolled out of bed and shuffled across the room. Peeping out of the heavy, purple curtains, and some way off, I could see Don, armed with a chainsaw; he was cutting back the tree that was spread over my collapsed chalet.

Putting on the dressing gown from the pile, which had been placed on a wicker chair, I surveyed the room. It appeared that I had slept on a sofa bed, in what I then saw to be some sort of therapy room.

There were four small tables covered with candles, a massage bench stood folded in one corner and, on the walls, many framed certificates; all bearing the name Rachel Moore. Apparently, she was qualified in Indian head massage, Reiki, hypnosis, past life regression, herbal medicine and reflexology; I thought this was handy, as I probably needed all of these. Above the bed there hung a large framed poster, of an image I recognised instantly. It was the Alistair Crowley tarot card, the sun; a positive sign. I was not a card user myself but had been around the long-gone Kensington and, still bubbling, Camden Lock Markets enough, in my many-shaped pasts, to have seen this before.

I recalled a morning at Camden Lock, many years before, when I was setting up my stall, and a young woman asked me if I knew where any card readers were. I directed her to a place in the market where she would find one. The next morning another woman appeared, this time offering me a reading; notably, she did not suggest this to any of the other stall holders. Quite miserable at the time, I told her I did not want one; she, nonetheless, told me this was fine, but that she could see many plates spinning and showed me the sun card. I did not welcome this attention.

I believed that it was probably a courtesy call, from the tarot reader who I had sent a client to, but this troubled me for some time, and still did.

Back to the present, and with my banging head, I went to the ensuite bathroom, carrying the rest of the items left for me, and was shocked to see that half my face was black and blue; I hadn't got off so lightly.

I made myself as respectable as I was able to, given the circumstances, and headed out into the sitting room, where I was greeted by the sight of Rachel, straddling a yoga ball, with her hands stretched towards the ceiling. For a late sixty-something, she didn't look bad in her lilac active wear.

"Good morning, Alice, love," she sighed, in a release of breath. "We did check up on you, once or twice, and you were out for the count". Well, this was endearing, if slightly disturbing; the thought of being spied on in my slumber wasn't something I was used to.

"Thank you," I slurped, through my swollen chop, trying to smile but probably making a spectacle of myself, if the look on her face was anything to go by.

"Oh my goodness, that does look painful," she cringed.

If this was her business, she might have wondered if I could have been thinking about suing them, but for some reason I didn't think the possibility had even crossed her mind. I wouldn't anyway; I was in no mood for such formalities.

"Do you think you could manage some breakfast, perhaps some scrambled eggs and tea? I think orange juice might be a bit sharp for you today. Just give me a nod dear, I don't think you should try to talk too much," she said, smiling again.

I nodded, and tried not to smile.

"You just relax, sit yourself down and I'll be right back," and off she rolled on her ball, in a sort of butterfly stroke maneuver. I didn't sit down; instead I took the opportunity to have another look at the photos on the wall.

There we all were, my dad, mum, brother and me; with lots of other happy faces. In one of these I was wearing the little cowboy suit that I'd had a couple of Christmas's before; it was by then, a tad short in the leg department. Everyone was in some sort of Western get-up, even the flying Bobby had a kerchief tied around his neck.

I had a vague memory of that day. I saw that Rachel was standing next to me at the end of the line, and Don had his arm around my dad; they were laughing. I could clearly take it that they were close friends.

I began to wonder when I should make my identity known. I realised that my sore mouth was a bit of a blessing, as I had a good reason for not saying too much; and they would have no idea the photos meant anything to me. With no reason for their being able to put two and two together, I decided to bide my time.

I sat down on the rather nice Chesterfield sofa just as Don came through the door. "Hello girl, how are you doing today?"

Why I felt guilty when I had nearly been taken out by a tree falling on me the night before, I did not know; except that I always felt guilty, and I was, sort of, sneaking around in their bungalow, and otherwise. "I'm fine, thanks," I said, smiling my lopsided smile again.

"Good Lawd, look at your poor face! Rachel will sort you out, don't you worry my girl," he gasped, looking very concerned. I must have appeared quite a sight. "You'll have to stay with us a few days, until we get you fixed, and we'll pop you in another chalet."

Oh Lawd, I thought, I didn't know what my little self had been up to but had the distinct feeling that it was something to be embarrassed about.

"I've been thinking, I have just the song for you on my jukebox," Don said, grinning broadly at me. After showing me a tin full of old coins, he placed one in the slot, tapped in the numbers and White Rabbit by Jefferson Airplane started to play. He then swayed to the rhythm in a trance, oblivious to just how apt the lyric 'ask Alice' was.

The tin of coins made me think back to my little pocket. One of them would have been the kind of thing I would have tried to acquire and pop in there; to add to our evidence. We would never have taken real money, or anything of value, although I think we would have considered one of these coins acceptable; as they were merely being used as tokens. I found it impossible to remember anything we did actually collect.

Rachel called from the kitchen; breakfast was ready. I was, by this time, very hungry indeed. Eating was no easy task though, I soon realised. Don, seeing me struggle, kindly suggested that taking a mouthful of tea with my food might help it go down. I took him up on the idea, as I was keen for the meal to be over with and to get out of there for a while. When we had finished, we all went to the chalet to collect my belongings. It didn't look as bad as I had imagined it would; Don having cleared the branches and making a start on sorting out the roof; yet it was still not really habitable.

With my things back at the bungalow, I got ready as quickly as I could and said I was going into the village. Rachel insisted on applying one of her herbal remedies to my face and recommended a Reiki session before dinner that evening. This was kind of her, and made me feel very guilty about my deception. I had also begun to feel concerned that if they had access to the details of visitors they would recognise my surname. I didn't even know why I felt this would be a problem but hoped I could know more before this happened.

As I left, I hatched my plan. I wanted to visit the big house, hoping it might jog my memory, and wondered if the local library might have any old newspapers from those times. I headed purposefully out of the gates when, almost directly opposite the caravan site, I was stopped in my tracks. On the other side of the road, I found it impossible to think that I hadn't noticed this before, there stood a house I then recognised. It was now run down but its Arts and Crafts architecture was remarkable. I also knew that I was familiar with the inside; I put this thought in my little pocket and kept on walking. I had set my mental Tardis to nineteen sixty nine.

I was now Liz, the Doctor's assistant; the scientist. I would be methodical, unemotional and fearless; this meant avoiding being Alice as much as possible. It was going to be hard, as I also needed little Alice's memories.

Given that it was a pleasant day, and about twelve o'clock, as I approached The Inn, I was surprised at how quiet the public garden was. In my memory, it had always been packed at this time of year. The car park, however, was full. This didn't make any sense at all, until I saw the long queue of people outside the big house. I decided to join it. Call it synchronicity or good fortune, if you will, but I was in the right place at the right time.

The middle-aged woman in front of me was complaining to a man, who I assumed to be her husband, that she didn't want anything small round the back or in the basement. From this I fathomed that the development was going ahead. As I reached the front of the line, I saw men in hi-visibility jackets asking each visitor questions and understood that I might have some difficulty in gaining entry.

"Can I have your invitation please, madam?" I hated being called madam.

"What invitation?" I replied, trying to appear outraged. I could hardly look at him; instead my eyes were on the building, and felt it beckoning me in.

"You must have one to visit the site?" He was agitated and waved his clipboard at me.

"Look here, I've come all the way from London. I was just told midday on the telephone, and I do not have an invitation, of any sort," I didn't like lying, but it was necessary.

"How old are you?" he replied, looking amused at his own words.

"Well, that's charming, young man. How old are you?" Other words came to mind.

"These are potential retirement apartments; are you over fifty?" he mumbled through a smirk, winking at his colleague, which I found very insolent.

"I certainly am!" The state I was in, I must have looked, at least, a decade older.

"I suppose you can go in then," he gestured to the stairs and turned his attention to the next viewer.

"Well then, thank you very much!" I dropped Liz, and a few expletives, on the disappeared gravel drive, and became Alice again; tall or not.

Travelling through time and space, I mounted the first of two, once creamy, narrow stone steps beneath the weathered pediment and, nervously, made my way into the big house. Passing by the neglected black door with its familiar, central, octagonal knob, I was unable to resist the urge to stroke this.

There was the hallway, with grand, panelled doors on either side of a rounding, heavy wooden staircase; its turned spindles and handrail were known to little Alice. I ran my fingers around their curves and clasped the sleek wood. I believed I had slid down this, as I could, again, see things from a different perspective, in my mind's eye.

As I reached the first landing, a painted image, surrounded by elaborate plaster work almost sent me falling backwards. We had called him the Night Walker, my brother and I; his face, barely visible, beneath a wide brimmed brownish-black hat. He carried a scythe over his left shoulder, and wore a long, soiled tunic, with a pin-worked chest, and was followed by two large horses; one grey and one black, in the rural scene of a sun down. There had been a framed painting of the same character somewhere at The Inn, I remembered, without the horses; standing on his own in a moonlit field. Perhaps he was some ancient local, but to me, and my brother, he was a phantom.

We were convinced that it was he who chipped away at the flint stones of The Inn at night; he who had sat at the end of our parents' bed and set Bobby barking. We were woken up by the commotion.

A solution to the mystery of the falling stones was also a hot topic at my grandparents' house. From the other side of that perpetually closed sitting room door, we spent many an evening listening to the various theories. When at The Inn, we often resorted to sharing a bed at the times when this had originally happened and hid beneath the covers; we would hear scraping sounds and the chip, chip, chip of something working away at the exterior walls.

This was our story too and felt it our right to eavesdrop. In the mornings after these events originally happened, stones would be scattered close to the building, for all to see; leaving empty spaces in the grey mortar. We were never consulted on this at The Inn, or at our grandparents' house, even though they must have known that we knew this had happened.

'Could it have been animals?' someone asked, from behind the sitting room door. There was no reasonable explanation as to why they would; so that was a no. If that was the case, there would hardly be any left after more than two centuries. And, what sort of animal could chisel away such secure stones with their beaks or claws. There had also been the unmistakable sound of metal against mortar.

'Could someone have borne a grudge?' This drew the creepy suggestion that perhaps there was an aggrieved individual, who wanted to tear The Inn down, flint by flint, for some reason. We had nodded, simultaneously, at the foot of the stairs, believing this to be the work of The Night Walker, with an axe to grind.

Occasionally, I would try to bring the subject up over the fish and chip suppers, at my grandparents' house, but this was always brushed away with jolly memories of visits to The Inn by various family members. Once I shared my recollections of the hot pants competition, which my aunt had taken part in. This was also never to be discussed again, with us around, after I mentioned the girl in pink plastic hotpants - she had bolted from the toilets, screaming her way through the saloon bar; before escaping into the garden and falling over a large dog.

As I have said, my brother never remembered this stuff. But how could he have forgotten? He is two years older than me.

The person sitting at the foot of my parents' bed, well this had to be The Night Walker. There was no one else in the room except them, and our dog, Bobby, when they turned the lights on. I was sometimes next door, in my bedroom, and could hear all the barking, crashing about and muffled, raised voices. Once, my brother heard the commotion from his room and came into mine, to find out what was going on; we listened, ears pressed to the wall.

At our grandparents' house, during those hidden, sitting room conversations, it was finally agreed that these were supernatural happenings.

One incident there stuck me as most significant. I remembered swivelling around on the orange, nineteen-seventies, leather egg chair, which was somewhat out of place, as I sipped advocaat from a short glass bearing a hunting scene; after all those years I was still able feel its design with my fingers. I knew I had then asked, "Who was the man in the caravan, with the motor bike?" They all looked shocked at this, but said they had no idea who I was talking about. I knew they were lying.

Bringing myself out of my thoughts and turning on the landing of the big house, I was faced with double doors; I opened them and entered the room with a view. Three tall windows overlooked The Inn, the gatehouse, the village green and beyond.

Mrs Napper could walk but she was unsteady. When in this room, with the plants on the tables, I would wheel her about in an ancient wicker bath chair. Those tables were gone, as was she, but I could still discern their footprints on the oak floor boards, marked out by the over flow from careless watering having trickled down their legs, all those years ago.

She seemed very old to me at the time, but I couldn't put an age to her. Sometimes we would listen to music, played on an antique horned gramophone; I was allowed to turn its handle. Although, I would imagine that the machine was from the nineteen twenties, I couldn't be sure what her relationship to it was.

My mother always maintained that all that watering, winding and sharing of chocolate gingers was a way into the outside world for Mrs Napper, through my little blabber mouth. I didn't doubt that this was probably true, in some sense, yet I knew that if I was the housebound Mrs Napper, I too would have made the most of this opportunity.

In truth, at least during my early visits, it was she who shared information with me; I wished that I could remember it all. I did recollect her telling me that the room with the plants had been was used for balls and parties. The walls were partially panelled in a dark wood and there was much fancy plaster work around the ceiling, in which I could see damage at the point where a chandelier had hung. Its huge mahogany fireplace had also, sadly, been removed since I was last there.

We would look out at the car park and she would describe the ladies riding side saddle, with bowlers or top hats; nets pulled down over their faces, as their horses pawed the ground, eager to be away. There were dray horses, crunching the gravel beneath their enormous feet, when delivering beer to The Inn; wearing polished black and gold harnesses. All manner of thing she had witnessed over the years, through these very windows. Sometimes, if I was lucky, we would have a look at a few of the other rooms. As I have already said, most of those I saw were unused and unfurnished by then.

After a while I headed back, through the landing, passing beneath a low archway leading to a long corridor, along which a series of doors faced each other; all open.

I saw the woman from the queue, still looking displeased, now complaining that her companion couldn't work out which rooms would be sun-filled in the morning. There is no satisfying some people, I thought to myself. The one I found them in had an inglenook fireplace, which they both had begun to study intently.

"What on earth are these marks? Something has been scratched into this," she said, appearing even more indignant, despite the fact that this room, nor any of them, belonged to her as yet. I didn't like the idea of her living here at all, and pictured her shoes disappearing up the chimney.

I went over to have a look myself and felt smug on announcing that they were marks made to ward off witches.

"How horrid, do they still have witches in Norfolk?" she asked, looking shifty as she spoke to her companion, ignoring my presence.

"I suppose, they might do," I added, smiling my scary smile at no one in particular, before heading to the next room. I felt protective towards the building and had a sense of respect for all the others who had trodden those boards previously; this was my past also. I wanted to be normal for Norfolk, and had a feeling that I might have been, once.

Looking around the other empty rooms, I found that those still with fireplaces had similar markings on them. At some point in time, the inhabitants must have been very worried about things that went bump in the night.

I was mesmerised by the grand house, travelling along the staircases and corridors. After all my years of trying to remember, I relished the atmosphere of each space I entered, rubbing my hands on surfaces, drinking in the odour of dust and old wood. I stood at windows, oblivious to the other viewers, and tried to pull back memories from my childhood; attempting to create a picture of the past by dismantling the buildings which had sprung up alongside its walls.

I was particularly drawn to the space behind, where the caravan site had once been. This was somewhere we played all the time. We had a little camp of our own, that we had marked out by pulling up weeds enough to make a small track. We took abandoned beer crates there for seats, and used glass jars as candle holders on, very rare, night-time visits; when we wanted to spy on some of the caravan dwellers. Through the maze of the development, I tried to work out where this had been.

I knew it was very close to the hall at the back of The Inn, once used for concerts and wrestling. From my view, I could see that at least some of this had not been built on. It was still quite wild.

After this, I came upon and ventured down a small informal stairway, near the front of the building, which led me to, what I imagined to be, the servants' quarters. It was surprisingly familiar; I felt I had been in there many times but that I had, somehow, never thought of it as part of the main house. Although, it was clear that it had not been occupied for many years, the decoration was more recent than in any other area. I looked closely at the paint on the walls, where the cupboards and fittings had been removed; there were traces of a milky blue and creamy yellow around the ragged edges, behind the other coats painted on top of these since then. I could see this as a kitchen, in those colours, and also, more to the point, Rachel, one hand on the hip of her patchwork maxi skirt, pouring water from a red kettle with the other.

The image of a huge tan coloured dog sprang into my mind; a Great Dane. He had once put his huge paws up on my shoulders and knocked me clean into the un-lit fire place in the bar; much to everyone's amusement.

Through the window, next to the door, I saw the courtyard with brick kennels along one side; this was how it had appeared separate from the main building, I realised. It would have seemed like a little house in its own right, to a small child. There was nothing much else to see there, except a high wall, an elaborate metal turnstile and gate, with a bell hanging from a curled hinge at its top. I imagined hounds must have lived in the courtyard originally.

I turned back and tore off a small part of the loose paint, to satisfy the urges of the little pocket, and made my way back through that immense house, in the knowledge that it would now be even more vivid in my recurring dreams. I was glad of the chance to have seen it once more, in its entirety, before being broken up into little dwellings

Chapter Four
Suspicious Minds

Knowing that I would have to reveal myself to Rachel and Don, I went in search of gifts. There weren't many shops in the village. I also found that I would have to take a bus to the next town in order to visit a library, so I had to postpone my research. Instead I bought some bottles of beer, as I didn't see Don as a wine drinker, and a bottle of red, in case Rachel was; and a bunch of flowers. I clanked my way back to the site, my mouth and face feeling a little better. Don was busy at the entrance, hanging up a long PVC sign.

"Bloody council; only let us put it up on the night. They say it isn't in keeping with the rural image." The sign read, 'Haunted Walk, Tonight from 6p.m. All Welcome'. "Rachel's got a client in at the moment but she's looking forward to giving you the treatment."

"Thanks Don, this really is very kind of you both."

"Now, don't you worry; you go in and have a sit down. She won't be long."

I plodded off into the bungalow. From the sitting room I could hear the plinkity plonk swirl of tranquil music coming from 'my room'. I carefully arranged my purchases on the coffee table and made myself comfortable on the Chesterfield, resisting the desire to look at any photos; I was feeling quite tired and allowed my eyes to close for a moment or two.

Again, I saw my brother, this time as his eight-year-old self, with that plastic teapot; shushing, holding a finger to his lips and pointing at the passage entrance with his outstretched arm. I had a good mind to call him and ask what he did remember about things that went on at The Inn, but I'd brought this up several times over the years and always left the conversation feeling a bit of a twit.

The door to the therapy room opened, and I had to stifle a laugh, when the woman who had been at the viewing of the house appeared; looking less irritated but, by no means, serene.

"Well, hello!" I couldn't help myself and winked at her. "It's nice to see you looking so relaxed." Her hair was a bit skew-whiff and her skirt was caught up in her undergarments. I didn't know exactly why this woman bothered me, but she did. I would have to dig myself out of this one, as I wasn't sure if I wanted to tell Rachel where I'd been.

"You know each other?"

"We bumped into each other in the village, didn't we?" I blurted out.

"We certainly did," she replied. With this, and a small thank you to Rachel, she headed out of the door, adjusting herself; looking back at me in an unpleasant, knowing way.

"Oh, what have we here?" Rachel said, spotting the gift-bearing table and forgetting her client. "You shouldn't have; we're supposed to be looking after you!"

"They're just small tokens. Thanks for putting yourselves out. Listen to me, I can talk without slurping; it must be your wonder cream!"

"I told you it would work. Come on through; it's your turn now. We've got a busy night ahead, and you need to be at your best to keep up with it; you'll have a great time!"

Before I knew it, my face was planted through the hole in the, now unfolded, therapy table. The energy from Rachel's hands passed over my head, then down my spine, and I was lost in a bodily slump, as many colours swam before my closed eyes.

When the treatment was over, feeling rejuvenated, I made myself ready for what I imagined might prove to be a very interesting evening. I decided to let myself go with the flow. I had taken many walks but never a haunted one; well, not by prior arrangement, at least.

As I ate my meal of falafel salad, again, the canteen began to fill up with faces I had not seen on the site. Some were alone, there were a few family groups with older teen-age offspring, and the odd couple; one of these being the grump and her partner. A woman, of about my age, then asked if she might join me.

"I was on my way back from visiting the monkey sanctuary, when I saw the sign for the walk, and I couldn't resist it," she said, with a friendly smile.

"Are you staying on the site?" I asked.

"No, I'm at a holiday cottage in the village. I decided to have a little break on my own."

"So did I", I replied, happy to find a kindred spirit of sorts. Well, there was something, other than our age, that we had in common. She was much smarter in appearance than me, I felt quite shoddy by comparison to her sharply bobbed hair and modern hiking outfit, realising how stuck somewhere I was; I hadn't been moving forward at all.

It was just then that Rachel appeared, dressed in a very authentic looking Georgian mourning costume; high busted and in black satin, with a matching bonnet, decked out in ostrich feathers. Her imposing figure brought the place to silence, followed by a ripple of expectant whispering.

"Shall we begin our walk?" she spoke in a quiet, yet commanding voice and floated out of the door. I was impressed. I counted about twenty people making their way after her, along with myself and my new friend for the evening. We didn't have to go far before our first point of interest; it was the Arts and Crafts house across the road, which I had noticed earlier that day.

"Ladies and Gentlemen, you may be familiar with the Pre-Raphaelite movement, founded by William Morris and his brotherhood. This house was built by some of those, as a retreat from the Victorian squalor that was London, at the time." We all stood about, surveying the house, from behind the neglected wooden fence.

"You may also know that these artists were in the habit of taking young country girls, whom they recognised as particularly beautiful, and attempted to refine them through education, into ladies." I was even more impressed; she certainly knew her lines.

"A local girl, Iris Drew, the youngest daughter of a farming family, caught the eye of one of the visiting artists. She was a noted beauty, with an abundance of intensely rust coloured hair; so long that it passed her slender hips. At first the family were happy with the attention she received, then one day her father insisted on seeing the paintings, which by then had become more bohemian. Disgusted at what his daughter had become, he cast her out and she had nowhere else to stay except in this house; rejected by all who had previously known her. The artist moved on, and others came and went. She rarely ventured further than this garden, but one winter's night she took a walk back to the village, longing to see those whom she had loved. Turned away from every door, she made her way back in a terrible snow storm and was found the next morning, dead and icy cold on this very path." Everyone stared down at the path beneath their feet, looking genuinely sad at this tale.

"To this day, given the right conditions, she is sometimes seen making her dejected journey, back to this house. Only this January, a young man visiting our camp site returned in a distressed state, claiming to have seen a young woman in a long, snow covered dress walking some twenty yards ahead of him, and then disappearing by this very gate. He was so disturbed that he left the next morning but came back a week later, feeling the need to talk about it and revisit the place. Others claim to have seen her in the garden or looking out of that attic window." She raised a shining black arm and pointed dramatically at the weathered roof, "God rest her soul". A few voices mumbled a response of the same.

"And so, we continue our journey of sad souls."

As we headed off in the direction of the village, my companion could not suppress her admiration of Rachel.

"She's bloody good!" her face glowed in approval. "I don't know what I expected, but it wasn't this!"

"I know exactly what you mean," I offered. Despite being truly impressed by the show Rachel was putting on, I was, in fact, wondering where this walk might take us, and what I might learn.

We next stopped at a small pond, beside a tumbled down barn. "This is a very tragic and mysterious tale. During the Easter of eighteen seventy-one, a shepherd was tending to some lambs that had lost their mothers, inside this very building. His two-year-old son was playing outside with a small hoop and stick. When the shepherd came out to check on him, the child was gone. The pond and the entire district were searched, but they never found the child. Legend has it that a farm worker was seen passing this way, with his scythe hanging over his shoulder, but he was never identified." The Night Walker, I thought to myself.

"Sometimes people have seen a shepherd, in old fashioned costume, far off in the distance, looking in hedges and ditches. This story does have a strange twist."

She paused before continuing, "Many years later, a middle-aged man appeared in the village one day, showing himself only to the blacksmith at his forge and then the vicar in the graveyard, saying that he had been lost as a child and had come home. He was never seen again after these short exchanges. It was often wondered if he was not the shepherd's child. There have been many similar tales of people going missing around these parts."

It was dark, by this time, and we were getting closer to The Inn; right next to it, in fact. "As we venture along Beach Lane, I ask you to imagine the low sound of hooves covered in sacking, a common method used by the many smugglers who have passed this way; to disguise the sound of their presence, on nocturnal journeys to and from the notoriously treacherous bay." At that moment there was the unmistakable sound of a horse travelling at speed; we all looked down the road, and at each other, for confirmation that this was actually happening.

She continued, "One of these went by the name of Augustus Tilney, a hard-working man by all accounts, doing the only thing available to provide for his large family, when times were hard. As he reached this spot, his trusty horses were spooked by something; he was caught beneath the wheels of the cart and dragged all the way to the old church around the corner, where the animals came to a halt." We all flew to either side of the narrow lane as a coloured pony and trap went belting past us.

"Hold onto your hats, and don't worry about calling customs and excise; that was just a local lad exercising his trotter," she laughed. "As for poor Augustus, he was taken to Norwich assizes to be hanged for smuggling but died from his injuries on the way there." We all heaved an audible sigh of relief, but not for poor Augustus. "There is one very odd detail to this story; although he was to be convicted of smuggling, there was nothing on the cart when it was found." I wondered again, if the scythe bearing creature wasn't at the bottom of this.

"And now, if you please, turn to face The Inn itself. Many visitors, and its occupants, have heard the sound of the rampaging cart and horses making their way by here on moonless nights."

As the group turned to face its stony exterior, I was already eyeing up my old bedroom windows. "But this is a minor happening, when compared to the other sinister events at The Inn on the Green," she said softly, again letting out a little sigh.

Walking around the flint wall surrounding The Inn, I braced myself for what would unfold, suspecting that I might find something of myself in the story about to be told. It was, indeed, a moonless night, and the atmosphere was becoming increasingly creepy.

"Behold the façade of The Inn; if you look closely enough, you may discern spaces where stones are missing, due to no accident or deterioration. The night-time removal of the flint stone has happened in two eras; the first of these being when The Inn on the Green was the stables and coach house to the splendid Georgian residence, you will notice, at its rear."

"On the first instance, grooms, living in the loft, could hear the chipping away of the stones at night. They even resorted to taking turns, keeping watch, to catch the culprit, but were always unsuccessful. The horses were so unsettled by this that some of them became too dangerous to ride." I knew what was coming next.

"The second instances occurred in the period of 1969 to 1970, when the license holder of The Inn, and his family, would be woken by the sound of the chipping away of the stones, only to find them scattered at the foot of the building in the morning. Again, when a watch was kept, no culprit was ever found." I knew this to be true.

"As I have indicated, The Inn and the surrounding buildings are, in fact, the most common sites for ghostly incidents in the village." Well, this was no surprise to me, but my companion began to look very anxious.

"I'm staying over there, in that gatehouse," she was no longer glowing, but looked distinctly ashen; even in the dimmed light cast by the pub garden. "I thought it was just me, that I was tired, but there is something unpleasant about that place."

I followed her eyes, to the small house standing on the edge of the beer garden, but said nothing.

We were interrupted by Rachel. "Now we will take a short break for refreshments. Let us visit The Inn on the Green, and enjoy a little stiffener, or rehydrate ourselves, before we continue.

May the spirits be with you," she said, taking a courtesy before leading us down the path.

It seemed odd being in the bar at that time in the evening; I always saw it by daylight. I would have been in the rooms behind or upstairs by now. I longed to lift the counter and go back there, to my former home, as it was then; with Bobby sniffing around, and all our furniture.

I could picture my grandma in the bathroom, and remembered my nana joking about me eating pickled onions, like sweets, in the sitting room. Everyone came to visit us there.

I was drawn out of my memories by my companion, "What would you like to drink?" When I lived here, my answer was always a snowball or a shandy. It's funny to think that, as a six-year-old, I was often bought one of these by the regulars; well, it was the tail end of the nineteen sixties.

"I'll have half a pint of one of the ales, I don't mind which. Thank you."

We took our drinks to a table by the fireplace where, again, I caught a flash of myself with the Great Dane.

"How awful of me, I still haven't introduced myself. I'm Alice."

"I'm Susan, pleased to meet you." At this, we both laughed for some reason.

"So, Susan, what brings you to these parts, other than wanting to get away on your own for a bit?"

"I've never been to Norfolk before, so I thought it would be an adventure. Once I'd searched for 'holiday apartments to let', suggestions kept on popping up every time I went on my computer. The gatehouse came up one day and it was just the kind of place I was looking for; I don't drive, and it's very close to the train station. So that was it, and here I am."

"That's, more or less, how I arrived too. How long have you been here?"

"Oh, just a few days; I've spent most of my time walking, and visiting the places suggested by the tourist board.

"I hate to ask, but you mentioned that the gate house felt strange?"

"Well it does; I often feel that I'm not alone in there and, since I've been here, I've had strange dreams every night," she said, looking around suspiciously.

"Really, do tell me more!" Well, this was interesting, I thought.

"I keep dreaming about long corridors of empty rooms." I could hardly contain myself and had to hold back my willingness to divulge everything.

"Do you think they could be because you are next to the big house? Perhaps, on seeing it, your mind is trying to make sense of what's inside, and this has just been played out in your dreams?"

"That is a likely possibility; I hadn't thought of that," Susan said, not looking altogether convinced.

"And then, the feeling of not being alone. Well, it's a very old building. Whenever we go home, we feel our own presence in there. In an old place, surely something of the people, who had been there for many years, however long ago, might still be present?" This was probably how I made sense of things as a child.

"You could be right there; but I can't help wondering who those people were, and what they were like. It's not a very pleasant atmosphere."

"Has anything, more than the dreams and sensation, actually happened?" I asked, hoping for something exciting.

Susan was opening her mouth to speak, when Rachel tapped her glass with the ice tongues.

"Attention ghost walkers, could you please join me by the bar?" and we all made our way over. I found myself standing next to the grump.

"That wasn't long; I haven't even finished my drink," she complained. "I need to spend a penny, before we start off again."

I remembered then, that in our floor board searching for spy holes, we had, inadvertently, come upon the spot over the ladies' toilets. Once we realised this was the case, we agreed it was out of bounds. As I may have mentioned before, we were Catholics.

Chapter Five
Touch Me

"During the late Victorian era, when the front building of the stables was converted into a small bar, with stage coach and private horses still housed at the rear, there were several brewers in the village competing for trade. The main two being Watlings and Pulfords; they worked tirelessly to produce the best ales. Searching far and wide, for new methods, Pulfords, noticing the success of brewers from the north of the country, began to use the new railways to import some of their ingredients; one of these being barley malt from Bostock & Company." I saw some of the gathered ghost walkers tuning out, whilst others wondered where this was going and listened, waiting for the interesting bit.

"Queen Victoria was very popular with the people of Norfolk; Sandringham being a home to her heir, Prince Edward. Her eighty-first birthday, in nineteen hundred, being the cause for great celebration around the country and county, much ale was quaffed at The Inn on this event. In their efforts to make their product the tastiest, Pulfords had added far more malt than was usual. It was eventually discovered that arsenic was present in this component. Victims of this contamination, in other parts of the country, suffered debilitating symptom, but with such large amounts having been used by Pulfords, many of their beer drinkers died of poisoning." This sounded very sad but I failed to see how this would lead to a haunting.

"As we have already experienced, examples of manifestation do not always take the form of shadowy figures. In this case, it is by something, in other ways, truly unpleasant. On occasion, visitors to The Inn have remarked on the sound of belching behind them, when no-one is present. In one extreme case, the entire bar was evacuated due to an overbearing odour of excrement. Make of this what you will, but this is symptomatic of arsenic poisoning."

"Susan, do you think the word arse might be a derivative of arsenic?" I whispered.

"The mind boggles!" she replied, stifling a giggle.

"Did she really need to include this one?" the grump asked, to anyone listening.

"And now; to things that go bump in the night!" Rachel continued.

I was all ears.

She cast her pointed finger along all present, eventually resting it at me, "Have you ever felt that there was something in the room with you?" I got the idea that I was expected to participate in this theatre.

"Yes, I have," I called out, and I wasn't making it up.

"You are not alone then," she winked at me. "In the year of nineteen sixty-nine, the landlord of The Inn called in paranormal investigators, after many disturbances." Well, this was news to me. "They became very interested in strange happenings, and spent several weeks here, using the gatehouse as their base." Susan gave me a nod, with raised eyebrows. "They were present at the, still, locally notorious hotpants competition".

"This event had drawn young women from all over the surrounding area, as there was a prize of £20 from the brewery, and a photographer from the Eastern Press was due to attend." I had never forgotten that day, sometimes having little flash backs to it; it was special in some way.

"Everyone was enjoying the day; the winner had been chosen, and the prize giving and photo shoot were just taking place, when one of the contestants ran screaming through the saloon; coming from the ladies' toilets. In her haste to escape the building she fell over a Great Dane, just outside that door, and broke her wrist. She claimed to have been sent into a blind panic by a terrifying whisper, repeating 'I know who you are', over and over again."

As I mentioned, we had discovered a hole above these toilets but we did not use it and, I have to say, you could seen nothing more than the floor by the door from above, but as I saw this drama unfold, I knew I was not up there. I also remembered that my brother was hanging around the photographer the entire time, intent on getting at least a hold of the enormous camera.

"The four paranormal investigators positioned themselves in different areas after every closing time. One of them even spent the night with the landlord and his wife, in their bedroom. He too heard the scratching at the flint stones outside and was able to record, on a reel to reel tape machine, foot steps moving about the room." I had no recollection of this, at all. I don't suppose I was told who 'the investigators' were; as I have said, everyone visited us at The Inn.

"Another of the investigators nodded off in the public bar one night and woke up alarmed to see that the tables and chairs had been re-arranged." We all cast a suspicious eye over the furniture.

"Now, if you will follow me out into the garden - being careful not to fall over any sleeping dogs!" We all laughed.

"I was at school with the daughter who lived at The Inn then," announced the grump. I was speechless. "She drew something odd, and the nuns gave it to the priest; well, that's what my mum told me." This I did not remember. "She was quite odd herself; I don't think I liked her very much."

And I felt sure I didn't much like her either, if she was anything like her grown-up self.

Again, I put my faith in Jesus, Mary, the Doctor and Liz, this time in the hope that they might protect me from her recognising me; and if they couldn't do this, I wished that the Tadis would appear and take me back to the summer of nineteen-sixty-nine, where I could do something uncatholic to her little self.

"Oh?" Rachel spoke quietly, moving closer to her, looking quite scary in that get up, in the dark. "Well, I knew her as well, or have you forgotten?"

This was a temporary victory on my part; the grump looked quite embarrassed. Then I felt equally awkward, knowing that Rachel didn't know I was back.

"That would be me then," I announced. What the hell, I couldn't keep this up any longer.

"Alice!" Rachel looked me up and down. "I should have known; I thought there was something familiar about you."

"I'm sorry, Rachel, I really wasn't sure about you either, until tonight." This was a relief, "How funny!" All the other ghost walkers looked bemused, including Susan, and the grump.

"There has been a change of plan, everybody; with the surprise appearance of our guest ghost, I think we should make our way back inside The Inn on the Green."

Chapter Six
Come Together

"Would you mind speaking to everyone, Alice? I'm sure they would be very interested," Rachel was quite shy in her request, and I didn't see how I could refuse.
"Of course, I don't mind. Try shutting me up," I said laughing, rather hysterically.

I was first at the bar, buying myself a pint, probably not a good idea, but I needed one; and vodka and tonics for Rachel and Susan. When the group was settled, Rachel asked me to share my memories of living at The Inn, and the ghostly happenings.

"I have to say that I loved living here. It always seemed to be summer in my memory, although I know it couldn't have been, as we were here for a year or two." I could feel myself rambling. "As far as the ghostly stuff goes, I didn't think too much about it until I was older, and still don't know much about it all, apart from the things I was involved in. I remember the stones, and the hotpants competition, but I always thought the girl had been stung by a bee." I was getting a bit creative, as I didn't want to give too much away; to anyone.

I continued, "I had no idea about the paranormal investigators, partly because there were always visitors; usually, our family or people from the brewery. Plus the fact that, I'm sure few parents would alert their small children to these things; mine certainly didn't." I could see Rachel's eyes, pleading with me for recollections of something otherwordly.

"I do remember sometimes waking up to the sound of the dog barking and growling, coming from my parents' room. And, there was also the morning that I woke surprised to find myself in the sitting room, covered on the settee with my sleeping brother, and my parents, who were also asleep, in the arm chairs; despite the fact that we had all gone to bed upstairs, as usual." This seemed to please the walkers, and Rachel.

The grump then asked, "Don't you remember the picture you drew?"

"Oddly enough, I don't but then that's me all over; odd," I smiled at her, revelling in the moment; the beer had probably gone to my head by then. "While we're remembering; what's your name, and then I'll see if I can't recall anything about you."

"Judith, I was Judith Cunningham then."

"No, that doesn't ring any bells, I'm afraid," I answered, lying.

The little cow; I did remember her. One day, when we left school and were walking to catch the bus, I can hardly believe we did this at that age, but we sometimes did, we came upon a patch of daffodils; she told me that eating them made your hair grow thicker. Mine was always on the flimsy side, so, of course, I ate one, and was violently ill when I got home. I knew she had played a horrible trick on me. She was always mean; mocking the fact that I lived above a pub. I hoped that one of my ghosts would belch in her sour face.

Rachel asked, trying to change the conversation, no doubt, "Did you ever actually see anything?"

"Well, one night I was in my parents' bedroom, messing about with my mother's makeup. She had one of those dressing tables, with a large mirror, and one on either side; that you could move about. I was turning them, so I could see my profile, when I caught sight of what I thought to be a man, standing behind me, but when I turned around he was gone." The Night Walker, I thought to myself.

"That must have been quite an experience," one of the group commented.

"I was only five or six; I don't really know what I thought. It was all quite normal at the time; strangely enough. There's probably a lot I don't remember."

"On that note, I think we'll call it a day. Perhaps, if Alice remembers some more, we will have a very interesting walk next time."

Some of the group dispersed, while others bought more drinks, and I was left with Rachel and Susan.

"Susan is staying in the gatehouse," I volunteered, hoping for a reaction.

"And are you enjoying your stay?" Rachel asked. I could see she was expecting a negative response.

"No, I can't say that I am," Susan replied, looking a bit deflated.

"Do you think she could stay with us tonight, Rachel?"

"That's a very good idea. Would you like to go and collect anything you might need?" Rachel enquired.

"I don't think so," Susan shuffled about, trying not to make eye contact. I, however, was excited at the thought of learning what she had experienced.

"Oh, come on Susan, I'm dying to have a look in there." My identity was out and I was looking forward to exploring every inch of my old haunts.

"Alright then," Susan agreed, "let's get on with it."

We made our way through The Inn garden and car park to the little porch. The gatehouse was of the same beautiful red brick as the big house, yet in the dark it had a low, secretive look.

All those who had ever visited the big house would have been seen from here. I wished that buildings could talk.

As I remembered, the stairs were just inside the front door, but there was now no child gate at the top. We entered the sitting room, where there was a duvet on the settee, and next to this stood a small, purple suitcase; all packed up and ready to go.

"I see you've made yourself at home, then," Rachel said, in a kind, yet sarcastic tone.

"Why aren't you staying upstairs?" I asked. "You were going to tell me something earlier, I'd almost forgotten."

"There is no real reason, except that I just don't feel comfortable sleeping up there. I tried it and I didn't like it."

"Fair enough," Rachel said, not looking surprised by this. "Come on, let's go and have a look before we leave; I can see Alice is curious." She wasn't wrong.

Susan led the way. The stairs were made of a thinner oak than those in the big house but were still as ancient. The handrail was more recent, this was probably to meet with some safety standard or other. There was some wooden panelling, and the painted walls were sympathetic to the age of the place; the sitting room was a deep red, with the tiny hallway and the plastered areas of the stair walls a dark, matt green. Suitable as these were, they did make the place rather gloomy; as I felt sure it had always been.

Susan opened the narrow door that had been stripped of any previous paint or varnish. This led us into a long room, decorated in a flat, dusky pink; it was very nice indeed. The bed looked comfortable, draped in a grey, quilted spread. The other furniture consisted of a small wardrobe, drawers and a chair; all mahogany. Someone had made a good job in kitting this place out. When I looked closely at the fireplace, I could see the familiar markings, intended to keep out any passing witches.

"Perhaps you're a witch?" I asked Susan, regretting this as soon as the words left my mouth.

"What did you say?"

"Nothing Susan, sorry," I often speak before I think. "There are symbols on the fireplace surround; they're meant as a deterrent to witches.

She came over to have a closer look. "Oh, I see," she said, smiling, as her finger traced the curving lines.

"Let's go," Rachel commanded, as she swept towards the door. "You've seen enough for one night, Alice.

We must have made quite a spectacle, walking back to the camp site in the darkness; Rachel in her costume, and me with my ghoulishly bruised cheek. In the headlights of the few passing cars, Susan and I must have looked like we were travelling with a ghostly apparition.

As we arrived at the bungalow the rumbling bass of the Beatles 'Come together' drifted out of the windows. The song made me shudder; as a child the lyrics sounded quite sinister and reminded me of the strange stuff. The references to 'joo joo eyeballs' and the 'monkey finger' conjured up some disturbing images in my six-year-old mind; I didn't much like the idea of him 'groovin' up slowly' either.

Don was happy to see us all, including Susan; he didn't even ask why she was there. "Hello all, I was enjoying one of the beers from Alice and a few tunes on the old jukebox."

"We can see that," Rachel said, tutting. "Come here and take a closer look at Alice."

"Why, you're not worse are you luv?" he replied, looking concerned.

"No, she is not, just come here and look at her."

Don came over and began inspecting my face.

"Now, look at me, Don," Rachel put both her index fingers above her eyebrows, in the middle of her forehead and slid them to her temples, then down, straight passed her cheeks, and round to the nape of her neck, "Alice." I got it straight away, even if Don didn't.

Eventually, recognition spread over his face, in the form of a huge smile. "Well I never, if it isn't!

"Now, if you'd kept the same haircut, we might have known you sooner," Rachel laughed.

"Good Lawd, those were the days," he said, shaking his head. "Come and see this." We all went over to the framed photos on the wall. "Look, there's me and your dad; that was a grand event he put on there," he wheezed. "And there's you and Rachel," I pretended to be suitably amazed as he spoke. "She looks nearly as young as you do now," winking at me; winking, it seemed, was contagious in these parts. "Who's this lovely young lady?" he said, turning, and appearing to notice Susan for the first time.

"Susan is Alice's friend; she's staying at the gatehouse but is going to stop here tonight."

"Oh, right enough then," he looked a bit confused. "Well isn't that nice. We'll have a bit of a party; to celebrate."

"Maybe tomorrow, Don. I think it's been a long day for Alice." Rachel interjected, looking a bit tired herself.

"Oh, of course, you need your sleep, my girl. Get you fully mended."

Before long I was in the sofa bed, in 'my room', with Susan; Morcombe and Wise sprang to mind. When I told her this she said the exact same thing had occurred to her. We tried to remember the storyline of 'That Riviera Touch', but neither of us made it past the first trapdoor scene before falling asleep.

Chapter Seven
Bang Bang

After breakfast the following morning, when considering what to do, Susan decided she would give up on the tourist board attractions.

"I'll just come along with you, if you don't mind the company?"

"That's an excellent idea; we can work as a team." I was excited by the prospect.

"A team of what, exactly?" she said, looking perplexed.

"Time travellers; we can take a walk down my memory lane."

"Given what I heard last night, I think that might prove very interesting.

Susan seemed a suitable assistant, given that I was minus a Doctor, and I was glad to no longer be alone in the place, to be honest.

"There are two things I want to achieve today. I haven't really explored the village, so that's first, and then we will take the bus into Cromer, as I need to visit the library to do a bit of research."

Rachel and Don were busy with their work on the camp site, and I was looking forward to seeing them later; wondering what I might be able to find out at our party. Before I heard their side of things, I wanted to see what else I could work out for myself, though. For all those years, there had been an air of secrecy about this time in my life; I felt that there was a mystery to be solved and that no one was going to, or could, give me the full details about it.

Having seen The Inn and the other buildings, I wanted to find out what the rest of the village had to offer. We walked around many lanes, most of which meant nothing to me. Although, the vicarage stirred a memory of something that seemed important; I then remembered that this was just a bit of a shaggy dog story.

Bobby had become friendly with a group of builders who had been coming to The Inn every afternoon for lunch. One day, I decided to clean his greasy collar and was in terrible trouble when he then went missing, with nothing to identify him. I was grief stricken at the loss of my friend. It wasn't until that evening, and after much searching by everyone, that the vicar found him, on returning home. He had followed the builders and become locked in the vicarage, where they were working. Now, this seems trivial, in itself, but it reminded me of something else. Something about being lost, and then found. I then decided to see if the short high street, facing The Inn, brought anything else back to mind.

I was disappointed to find that, despite the presence of the post office, many of the shops had changed hands, no doubt due to the arrival of a large supermarket on the outskirts of the village; this being the death knell to many a small business around the country.

Little independent traders had taken the place of the, then traditional, butcher's, bakery and hardware shops. One of these stuck me as interesting; it was called 'The Circle'. According to the hand painted sign, it was established in nineteen seventy. Its window was full of books on the supernatural, tarot cards, little trinkets and dream catchers.

"Do you think we should go in?" Susan asked.

"I believe we should," and a bell above the door tinkled as I pushed it open. A man and woman sat behind the counter, at the rear of the shop, huddled over a newspaper. They both wore embroidered velvet jackets, with tie-dyed shirts peeping out. The man had an impressive grey beard and she had very long, henna-red, wispy hair; a couple of sixty-year-old new age hippies.

"Good morning, do you mind if we have a browse?" I asked their still downturned heads.

"Feel free," the woman answered.

There was something familiar about them; but given their age, and assuming they were locals, they were probably people I'd seen before, perhaps, but this may have been since my recent arrival. They then kept a quiet watch over us, as we examined the items for sale. I came across a rack, by the door, with leaflets advertising spiritual retreats, healing centres and practitioners; weekends to explore your inner witch and many more. There was a whole industry going on here in the village. I felt our work here was done, for the present.

We then waited for the bus. "Now, I know I may appear a little mad," I said, and Susan nodded at this, "but, amongst other things, I know that someone died in the village at the time I was here. I think this might be important."

"I'm sure some people must have died when you were here."

"I don't mean the ill or the old; there are other kinds of deaths. My mother told me, only the other day, that one of the reasons we left was because someone had died. I just have the feeling that it wasn't a normal death."

I remembered being in the chapel at school. An elderly lady, who was a neighbour of the place, had passed away. We all had to pay our respects to her. On our way out, Judith Cunningham slammed the door in front of me, blocking my exit, and wedged it shut with something. I was left alone with the coffin. It took me a long time to work out that I could escape through the door at the side of the altar. I then had to make my way down the corridor that I dreaded most; this was lined with life size statues of Jesus, Mary, and some wounded saints. A letter was sent home to my parents, saying that I had hidden to avoid lessons. Judith was no friend of mine.

On reaching Cromer, we found that the library wasn't very modern, which I found comforting. It was a small building, attached to the back of an old church.

Newspapers could be viewed on microfiche; I set about this and sent Susan in search of anything of interest to be found in the local history section. Suppressing my innate curiosity, I then flicked past the many pages of church bazaars, ancient archaeological finds, and Norfolk step dancing competitions.

Eventually, I came upon an article introducing my father as the new landlord of The Inn. This was a familiar sight. Every time we moved, which was every couple of years or so, he would appear, smiling and bow tied, in the local paper of our new home town. When I thought about it, I realised that although we changed locations frequently in my early years, because my father always ran places of entertainment, we were central to wherever we moved to. We instantly became part of things and became known to mostly everyone. Years later, he told me that when we arrived in London I used to say hello to anyone we passed in the street, as this was what I was used to.

I probably was a bit of an odd child, but this could not excuse Judith Cunningham's beastly behaviour towards me. My overconfidence might also have set me up for other things that happened. I had always, in a way, felt like I owned the place.

"You might like this," Susan brought me back to the present with a small volume of photos and anecdotes, produced by a local history group. "Here's a nice one of the big house."

It was the image of a group gathered at the front of the building for a shooting party. They were all dressed in tweeds, some with guns broken open after their barrels, resting innocently over their arms. It was dated as 1945. Some of their names were listed beneath; one of them was Mrs Evelyn Napper. I scanned the faces of the women and recognised the look of intent in one of them; it was her. I have a few friends who are police officers and they also possess something about the eyes. They always look as though they are seeing everything. I wondered what, or who, she was on the lookout for.

"Brilliant Susan; that's amazing," I began to relate the tale of my former existence, in the hope that an outsider might understand why I found it all such a riddle.

"That lady is Mrs Napper," I said, stroking my finger down her outline. "She lived in the big house when I was a small child, living at The Inn. I used to visit her, quite often. We would talk; sometimes she would show me other rooms in the mostly empty house and tell me stories of its past. My parents were always a bit suspicious of her reasons for our friendship.

"Such a huge building must certainly have created a big impression on a young mind." She looked genuinely interested, and I was grateful for this. Other people's stories can be a bore to some; I'm a bit on the inquisitive side and enjoy the little details.

"Well, that's just it. I often wonder if I haven't let my mind run wild over the years. The whole place is somewhere that invites invention but the way my family have been so closed, to say the least, when I have tried to talk about our time here, suggests something more was going on. This has always made me believe that there really was a drama, that I was part of, but didn't understand."

"Was there really any need for a drama as a reason to go? I'd have thought the ghostly stuff was enough"

"I always felt a different tension growing, and the ghostly stuff was just a day to day thing by then."

"Perhaps to you, but not to your parents; surely they found it all a bit alarming?"

I had to say, "I don't know. Rachel and Don could be a good place to start. I'm feeling quite tired now, let's photocopy this and get back to the camp site; we've a small celebration to prepare for.

Chapter Eight
Everybody's Talkin'

On our way back we stopped off at a shop selling local produce, including ales and wines; I wanted to make sure that all mouths were well oiled for the evening.

When we arrived at the bungalow, Rachel and Don were sitting on the Chesterfield. They stood up, and shouted, "Surprise!" Both of them were wearing clothes I recognised. Don had on a Led Zeppelin T-shirt and Rachel wore her patchwork skirt. "We thought this might take you back," Rachel said, swishing the material around her legs.

Don went over to the jukebox. "Let's liven this up a bit," he said, before putting the money in the slot and tapping in his selection. The organ, flugelhorn, guitar, and brass section began to play the introduction to 'Sweet Caroline'.

"My Grandma's favourite," I said, flooded with emotion.

"Well, that was a good choice," Don smiled. "A lovely lady, I remember her well."

"Those were great times," he added. "Your dad brought a breath of fresh air to The Inn; you wouldn't believe how quiet it was before then. He certainly knew how to put on a show and shook up the whole village."

I felt quite proud.

"How are they?" Rachel asked.

"They're thriving, both retired now for many years."

"They stayed in the business then? Don asked, somewhat awkwardly.

"Not for much longer. They ran another pub for a while, when we first moved to London, but gave it up; wanting a more nine to five lifestyle."

"And who can blame them," Don said, with them both nodding. "It takes a lot out of a person, keeping a place going morning through night."

"I remember you both working there."

"Yes we did, and so did every other bugger in the village at some point," Don responded, shaking his head. "It was that busy, you needed all hands at the pumps, so to speak."

"What with the caravan site behind then and this one here, there were lots of customers in those days. The place became a real crowd puller," Rachel sighed.

"How did you end up running this place?" Susan asked. I'd almost forgotten she was there for a moment.

"It belonged to my parents. You must remember coming here, Alice?"

But I didn't remember this at all.

"Sometimes you used to help me in the shop, selling buckets and spades, and stuff. You even stayed here before."

I was shocked at how much I had forgotten.

"Did my brother stay here as well?"

"No, he sometimes stayed over the road, in the Arts and Crafts house; he went to school with one of the boys who lived there."

"I'm sure it was nice to have a night out, but why didn't we just stay at The Inn?"

"Well, some events were quite loud, and went on till late. They would have been too busy to keep checking on you upstairs."

This seemed odd. Every night in a pub must surely have gone on until closing time, which was 11p.m., although, I had since had some experience of lock-ins, where no drinks were supposed to be served after this time but they were; I felt sure my parents wouldn't have done this.

I wondered if it wasn't when the paranormal people were staying, or if there were some other activities I didn't know about.

"Where are my manners?" I remembered the booze. "Let's have a drink to celebrate."

"Oh, you shouldn't have, Alice. We still have most of the other bottles you bought"

"Well, here's some more. Don, get back to that jukebox, and hit us with some more sounds!" The music was taking me back, and that was exactly where I wanted to go.

"Come on Susan, now, you choose, my luv". It was nice of Don to get her to join in; I realised I was neglecting my new friend. I felt at home and assumed she did too.

"Yes, come on Susan, take a coin and make your choice!" I was interested to see what it would be.

"It can only be this one!" she said, as the machine whirled, and a single rose and landed on the turntable; Johnny Cash's 'My name is Sue'. We all found this very amusing.

"Excellent!" Don cried.

"This photo," I said, interrupting the festivities, "there are lots of us in the line-up. Who else should I remember?"

Rachel and Don looked at each other. "Like I said, most everyone worked at The Inn, back then. You stuck with us, most of the time; I'm not sure who else you'd recall? Now there, that's Alf, the cellar man. You'd know him," Don sounded relieved when he noticed this. "You were great pals; your Bobby used to do the rats for him, and he would take you over to the working men's club to play dominoes."

I did remember that; they were very nice to me in there. I always left with a prize; a box of chocolates or something. But I felt that I was being distracted by this, intentionally. I went over and looked closely at the photo. There were other faces I recognised.

"Who's this?" I said, pointing to a sullen looking man at the other end to the line; myself and Rachel being at the opposite end.

"Oh now, I'm not sure," Don answered, trying to sound casual. I was sure he was fibbing, "Do you Rachel, my sweet?"

"No, I don't recall him."

Of course she didn't, I thought to myself, saying instead, "I've just remembered what Susan found today, at the library in Cromer."

"I wouldn't have thought the library was the most exciting place to visit," Don said. "What were you girls up to in there?"

"We thought we'd have a look for old pictures of around here," Susan replied.

"Yes, and we found this lovely old photo of the big house and Mrs Napper." I took it from my rucksack and passed it to Rachel.

"Well, she wasn't so old then," Don looked along the shooting party line up. "And there's Alf's dad; looks like he was one of the beaters."

"Is Mr Napper there?" Rachel asked.

"It doesn't say, there are names underneath but his isn't one of them." I said, scanning the image with them.

"Do you remember her, Alice?" she continued.

"Yes, I used to visit her in the big house."

"Did she ever say how she ended up in that chair?"

I had a feeling where this was going, and it wasn't going to be pretty. "No."

"She was shot in the back; it could have been on that day."

"That's terrible!" Susan gasped.

"Enough of that, Rachel," Don stepped in. "Let's not bring the party down now."

"Fair point," she smiled and nodded. "What do you remember about the house?"

"Some of the rooms and corridors," I was thinking. "Oh, and didn't you live in the servant's quarters?"

"My, you do have a good memory. Actually, it was the butler's apartment but you were very close."

"I remember you had a garage, somewhere on the land at the back, Don."

"Is there nothing you don't remember?" he laughed. "It wasn't exactly a garage, but you might remember I kept my bikes in the old kennels in the courtyard."

"Well, that sort of makes sense now," I smiled. "But if you lived there, how did I come to be staying here?" I asked, bemused.

"My parents looked after you a few times, you knew them well enough," Rachel was still surprised at my not recalling this.

"I really don't remember that at all."

"I suppose it looked quite different then, the site was mostly tents at that time."

"Right then," Don announced. "I do believe it's time for some food, Rachel has cooked something special for you."

We all went into the kitchen where I could smell something warm and savoury. "I fried this earlier and have been keeping it warm in the oven." Rachel announced, producing a tray of chicken, in seasoned breadcrumbs. I had omitted to tell them that I no longer ate meat, but knew I would have to tuck in.

"Does that remind you of anything?" Rachel asked, as I took a tentative bite into the flesh.

"Yes, it does, Rachel" I replied, trying to ignore what I was putting into my mouth.

"That's the exact same recipe we used at The Inn, when you were a girl."

"Did it have something to do with the Western Day?"

"Yes, we'd started a new menu of American style food, and the day was a publicity event."

I cautiously took another bite, it did taste familiar. Its peppery flavour stirred up a memory of the little tenant's garden, to the side of The Inn, and Bobby, licking his lips, and shuffling on his bottom; looking hopefully at my food. I still missed him.

The after taste of the chicken then revealed a different memory from that day and began to leave a bad taste in my mouth. I would have to think about this later, as I felt this was not the time to go prodding Rachel and Don for more information.

After the food, we played more music and chatted about nothing of significance. Not exactly what I had hoped for, but it was a nice evening. We then took a walk around the site, and Don proudly showed us all the improvements he'd made over the years. He also took us to the storage barn I had seen him entering when I first noticed him. It did contain all the gardening, camping equipment, and tools, as I'd imagined, but he also used it as a garage for his collection of motor bikes. Again, I remembered the other man with a motor bike, but given the response I'd received from my family when I had asked about this person, I decided not to ask Don about him either; well not for the moment.

Don and Rachel then mentioned that they were expecting the arrival of a large group the next day, and were going to set up tents for them, in the back field, the following morning. They were a very hard working pair, particularly considering their age; Susan and I offered to help them. Given this, we all agreed that it was time for bed.

Before going to sleep I drew out a map of The Inn and the surrounding buildings; and wrote some notes on what I had remembered and found out so far. I thought this might help me put things together, and be a bit of a guide to my assistant. I also made a list of the things that interested me most. It read:

Who shot Mrs Napper and why?

What did I used to keep in my pocket; and in our collection (wherever that went)?

What were the late night events at the Inn?

What happened at the Western Day?

Who was the other man with a motor bike?

What did I draw that shocked people?

I then let my mind wander about the place; through rooms and down corridors, hoping to have an interesting night of dreaming. The chicken was, by then, swirling around my stomach; being an unexpected presence in there. Despite all my tossing and turning, and a bruised face, also not being conducive to a restful night, I must have drifted off at some point as I eventually shot out of bed, dripping in sweat. The Night Walker was back.

Chapter nine

Season of the Witch

I must have fallen back to sleep at some point, as I was dreaming about being in bed in my old room, watching a telephone wire swinging against the leaded windows, when I realised the sound was actually a tapping at the door.

I sat up as Rachel came in. "Good morning, ladies," she was dressed in green overalls, "I thought you might like a cup of tea to start the day."

With this kindly interruption, I had no time to bring my dreams back; which was a bit annoying. I thanked her, and we prepared for tent building.

We were quite useless at first, until we got the hang of it by watching Rachel and Don, expertly pulling and pitching. They were so organised, I admired them greatly. Before long, ten tents were set up around the perimeter of the field and Don began to neatly prepare the wood for a camp fire, in a dug out bowl at its centre.

"This looks very impressive," I offered. "Who's coming?"

"Oh, it's a regular group called The White Witches of Waltham," he said, in a very matter of fact way; like this was not something at all peculiar.

Given the witch marks in the big house, I found this very interesting. "And what, exactly, do they do on their visits here?"

"They breathe in the nature and the spirits, apparently, or so I'm told."

"Well, that sounds like fun," I added. "Have they been coming here for a long time?"

"Yes they have, right back to when Rachel's parents still ran the place."

"Well, I suppose there's a lot of nature, and more than a few spirits to take in around here. And I should know!" Don chuckled, as I said this.

I spotted Susan, hauling some water canisters along on a trolley, and went over to her. Speaking quietly, I said, "Look, I've had an idea. Things are going to be quite busy around here for them tonight. I think we should go and stay at the gatehouse."

"I knew you were going to suggest that," Susan replied, looking pleased with herself. "Well if that's what you want, but don't say I didn't warn you."

I wondered what on earth she believed would happen. But this was just the sort of thing I was hoping for; an event.

Some lines from a poem I had learnt as a child sprang into my mind; I knew I probably had the words wrong, but the gist of it was the same: 'Who are you? Who are you?' At the foot of the Midnight Stair; I cried above the owls below, 'Is there anybody there?'

I was in the mood to be spooked into my senses. If anything was going to bring back my missing memories, it would be a few good bumps in the night. "Come on Susan, let's go and get our things, and head to the gatehouse!"

"Well, I'm glad you find the idea entertaining because I don't."

"It will be fun, but we need to go shopping first."

"For a crystal ball, I suppose?"

"You're close."

We made our way to the village, and dropped our belongings off, before having a walk around.

"Let's go back to 'The Circle' and have another look in there."

"As long as you're not going to buy a Ouija board or anything else of that sort," Susan said, looking apprehensive.

"No, definitely not; well, not today anyway," I joked.

The bell above the door announced our arrival again. There were quite a few customers inside the shop, which had been completely empty when we visited it before. I thought they might have been some of the crowd expected at the camp site; they looked an interesting bunch. There was an abundance of purple and green, with some in combat trousers or long skirts. A few of the women had flowers in their hair; this took me back to the sixties.

I was crouching down, looking at a display of large candles on the floor, when I came face to face with the eyes and muzzle of a dead fox, hanging from the belt of a large stomached man. I lurched backwards and almost toppled over at the sight of it. Seeing this, the man stepped towards me, seemingly intent on confronting me with the poor creature.

"Are you threatening me with that fox?" I couldn't believe I was saying this.

He glared at me and put his hands on the hips of his filthy jeans, in an aggressive stance.

"Sod off!" I added, and walked towards the counter feeling a little shaken at my own response to the situation.

"Do you have any books on historical witching activity in this area?" I asked the henna-haired lady.

"We do have a few local history books, but don't expect to find much about witchcraft in them; it's quite a secretive business." She looked me up and down again before pointing to a small section of literature.

Despite her protestation, I noticed Susan browsing around the display of tarot cards, balls, and boards before glancing over at me with raised eyebrows, gesturing towards the door. I shook my head.

The books, I found, contained nothing Rachel's ghost walk hadn't told me; she had possibly got her entire script from them. The phrase 'normal for Norfolk' sprang to my mind again. Some consider this a reference to inbreeding, while the truth of the phrase is more than likely an unwillingness to tell the truth, or anything at all. Norfolk folk are often believed to be taciturn; tight-lipped. This must be true of many close-knit communities; it's surely a survival mechanism, I thought to myself.

I bought one of the books anyway, as I keepsake. I thought my parents might like it. As I was paying for this, I remembered the date 1970 on the sign.

"I see the shop has been here a long time," I said, in a deliberately nonchalant tone, moving my eyes about the place.

"Yes, we've been going a long while now," the henna-haired lady replied.

"Have you always been here too?" I continued, innocently.

"It's my shop; I started the business up back then," she said proudly, forgetting to be unforthcoming.

"I used to live in the village," I offered.

"Where was that then?" she asked, suspending the book in mid-air.

"Oh, at The Inn" I answered, knowing this would get a response.

"I hope you enjoy your visit. That will be £8.99 please," she responded abruptly, almost throwing the book in the paper bag, whilst looking into my eyes and trying to seek out what I knew.

"Thank you, we'll call again," I didn't know why I said this, but it just came out; as usual.

The bell sounded our exit, and, I imagined, a sigh of relief.

"Let's have a walk down to the beach, and then dinner at The Inn."

"A suitable plan," Susan agreed.

I hadn't taken that walk to the beach for many years. In my memory it was a long one, but in reality it only took about fifteen minutes. To a small child it must have seemed endless, as after the road-side of The Inn, there was only an old farm, followed by a few houses; the narrow lane to the sea then being flanked by fields and gorse. This lead to the coast, with no other landmarks to indicate the distance travelled.

Then, as we made our way down the steep, sandy track, I instantly recognised the outline of the beach shop, little changed by all those years, and again, we saw some of the recently arrived witchy clan; out of place next to the beach balls, kites and swimming rings, that hung about, like us, hoping for adventure. The bay itself appeared as treacherous as I remembered. Over the years, I had heard of the occasional fatality here, on the national news; when people had been caught out by how quickly the tide comes in.

We walked far along the beach, and I watched the tide, pushing into the many caves that nestled beneath its cliffs. I saw my brother, my aunt and myself clambering over the rocks, and back to safety. Susan and I then sat on the shingle for a long time, in silence, until I felt uneasy and decided it was time to leave. This hadn't always been a happy place; I could feel its danger.

Chapter Ten
Bad moon rising

On our way back to The Inn, the rear of the big house could be seen from a distance, and all along Beach Road. I considered how the inhabitants would have had very clear views of the surrounding area from all sides, which seemed significant.

It still felt strange, re-entering the Inn, as a customer and so much older. It was another lifetime, so much must have gone on in this place since I had been here, and much had happened to me in the years between then and now. I felt quite sad as I leant against the bar, waiting to be served. I pictured my parents behind it, knowing that it must have been hard work, whereas to me, as a child, it was one long holiday; apart from going to school. My dad was almost military in his routine; everything shone, even after the busiest of nights. I could see him testing the pumps, and holding up glasses of each of the beers; one by one, to check them for cloudiness or whatever else his expert eye could detect.

When I was a young adult, and started going to pubs with my friends, he would tell me not to go to certain establishments, as they served slops; the overspill caught in the trays when pulling a pint. He was horrified when I drank lager from bottles, warning me of vermin in the cellars that climbed over the crates. Bobby had been an efficient rat catcher, and even in old age you only had to mouth the word to send him into a frenzy of activity; searching for the non-existent creatures. A cruel joke played on him many times.

"Cheer up there, girl." I hadn't noticed that a man of about my age, somewhere in his early fifties, was waiting for my order. "What'll it be then?" he asked.

"I'll have half a pint of this bitter, and a vodka and tonic, please." I then saw shades of recognition passing over his face, as he eyed me up, whilst drawing the beer.

"Now then, you were with Rachel in here the other night. Yes, you were; I'm sure of it!"

"Yes, that was me," I answered, trying not to shuffle about on the other side of the bar.

"Aren't you the girl who used to live here?" he asked, looking entertained at the prospect.

"I certainly am. I'm Alice, who was once young here; and now I'm here, but no longer young." We both laughed at this, to my relief.

"Isn't that a thing?" He then thought for a moment. "I'm Larry, the landlord now. Well, you go and make yourself at home again, Alice, my girl."

"I will. Thank you very much." I answered, feeling a little awkward, as I teetered off with the drinks.

Making my way through the beer garden, I thought about being known as the little girl who had lived at The Inn, and wasn't sure if this was a good thing or not. I had lost the invisibility that middle age provides. I could no longer walk about the place in anonymity and understood that this might prove problematic to my research.

Susan was sitting staring at the gatehouse. "Did you bring a menu?" she asked. "I'm starving here!"

"Oh bugger, I forgot to ask for one," I couldn't believe I had forgotten; I was also in need of food.

"I'll go and get one; I hope their still taking orders," she tutted, striding off across the lawn.

I took out my phone, brought up the contacts menu, pressed 'Parents' and called.

"Hello," it was my dad this time.

"It's me"

"Hello, Me," he said, as usual.

"Guess where I am?"

"Your mother's already told me."

"Of course she has, but anyway, I thought you'd like to know I'm sitting in The Inn garden with a tasty glass of bitter."

"Very nice, but be careful there," his meaning was illusive, as I am never quite sure when he is being serious or joking.

"What do you mean, be careful?" I could then see him fluffing around at the other end of the phone.

"They can be an odd bunch," he paused. "Just watch yourself with the locals. It's not somewhere to go sniffing about."

"Now why would I be doing that? Anyway, I bought you a souvenir today; a book of local ghost stories."

"Are we in there?" he replied, sounding unmistakably serious.

"No, it's just old stuff."

"Well, keep in touch, I've got to go; we were just going out when you rang.

"I'll call again soon. Take care." Momentarily, forgetting my present situation, I was happy, thinking about them going out to one of their locals.

"And you. Don't forget what I said."

I then had a sinking thought; that call didn't tell me anything other than offering the usual note of caution. I was still hanging around behind that perpetually closed door. Just how many years was I expected to be careful for?

Susan returned empty handed. “There are no evening meals today, but he said as you’re a special guest they could knock us up a couple of Ploughman’s.

I thought this was very kind of Larry, and felt pleased that being known had some benefits. Before long he appeared with the food, and more drinks on a tray; including one for himself.

“This is on the house. I hope you don’t mind if I join you for a break,” he said, settling himself in on the bench, next to me.

“Not at all, this is very generous of you Larry,” I replied, thinking I could take this opportunity to ask him a few things.

“So, you’re staying at the gatehouse?” he asked Susan.”

“Yes, I’ve taken it for a short break,” she replied. “I suppose you must have seen me coming and going?”

“I have, you’re the first of the season.”

“I’ve been staying at the camp site, on Cart Lane, but I’m going to spend some time at the gatehouse now.” I said, wanting to see what his response to this would be.

“I hope you’re not going to bring your ghosts with you,” he smiled and winked.

“My ghosts, I didn’t know that I had any?” I said, shocked by this, having imagined that I was going to be leading the conversation.

“Well, there haven’t been many since you left the place.”

He had answered my question, but if he was telling the truth, I found this difficult to believe.

“How long have you been here?”

"About five years now, and there's not been so much as a creaking floor board," he answered, taking a long drink of his pint. "Of course, some say it's because there are no children about the place."

"Are you telling me that the locals believe that all the stuff that went on when we were here was because of me and my brother?" I didn't know what to make of this.

"I suppose I am, as that's what I've heard," he finished his beer. "Enjoy the gatehouse; Rachel and Don have done it up very nicely."

Susan and I looked at each other, but said nothing. At this, he made his way back inside.

"I don't understand", Susan said, looking confused.

"Neither do I," this was a turn up for the books. "Who did you say you rented the place from?"

"I booked it on-line, it was through a letting company and the key was in a coded security box by the front door. I didn't meet the owners."

We finished our meal and took the tray back inside. I wanted to thank Larry again and ask him about Rachel and Don owning the gatehouse, but there was just a young barmaid looking after the place; he was no where to be seen.

"Let's have a walk about the buildings, before we settle in for the night." I wanted to have a look around the rear, at where our little camp had been. I was still amazed at the development behind the big house; it was hard to picture what had been there before.

I found the overgrown patch, behind the structure at the back, where the wrestling and gigs used to take place. It wasn't a very large area now, perhaps it wasn't then. We could no longer walk through it, as even as children we had to do a bit of gardening to keep our small path clear. What I really wanted to see was what our view had been from there.

I remembered the afternoon when my brother and I were disgusted to find that some creature or other, man or beast, had been to the toilet on one of our wooden crates. We thought that it had been left as a message, warning us off.

From here we could see the rear of the big house, and much of the, former, caravan site. I felt sure that we were suspicious of some of the people who stayed there. They were probably seasonal workers, as in my memory they weren't holiday makers; spying on them was a major occupation of ours. I remembered that sometimes we would take a cautious walk between the caravans, where our view was obscured; looking for evidence. I pictured a motor bike parked outside one of these and knew that its owner had been one of our main targets.

I squatted down, trying to recapture the scene as it had been.

"What the hell are you doing now?" Susan asked, looking at me, amused by my stance.

"Just having a better look at things," I didn't bother to explain why.

We walked back round the side of the big house and looked at the wall, to the butler's apartment. I tried to turn the elaborate iron turn gate, but it was padlocked, and then attempted to open the gated door next to this but this was also locked and wouldn't budge.

"You're not going to break in, are you?"

"No, I'm just trying to remember something." Again, the image of the Great Dane jumped into my mind. I could see his huge, tan coloured body, snoozing in the sun by the door. His big, kind face was resting on his enormous paws.

The gate was of interest to me. I remembered seeing it, from the butler's house, with its curled spring and bell. I had probably enjoyed making this ring in the past. "Come on, it's time for bed." My brain hurt from too much information, and calling to Susan, I felt the gatehouse beckoning.

"Brilliant, I can't wait!" Susan sighed, in a sarcastic tone.

I had never been inside the gatehouse at night time, apart from the evening before, as far as I could recall. It was already getting dark when we opened the front door, which was at the side of the building, next to the entrance of the drive up to the big house. I noticed the key safe; this reminded me of Rachel and Don. I wondered again why she hadn't told us that they owned the place.

Even with the light on, the small hallway and staircase were quite gloomy, with all the wooden panelling and small areas of period green paint.

"I don't like this," Susan said, looking genuinely scared. "It feels like someone has been in here. I'm sure our bags have been moved."

"You're imagining things. It's probably my fault, with all my searching for clues of things that probably don't amount to anything." I was lying. I knew I had left my rucksack on the armchair, and it was now on the floor.

"Do you want to stay upstairs, and I'll stay down here, or the other way round?"

“I think I’d prefer the Morecambe and Wise or Laurel and Hardy arrangement; we both either sleep up there,” she said, nervously pointing to the floor above, “or down here.”

“Well, in that case, I vote for upstairs. It will be far more comfortable, and I’m knackered.” And I was.

So, we went to bed. I was anticipating an excellent night of dreaming after all the cheese and pickles. I wasn’t to be disappointed. I was enjoying one of my favourites; which involved living in a small place and then realising that there were doors to other rooms which I could not use. When I remembered them, the rooms always seemed to hold something scary, and were in a state beyond my ability to return them to a habitable condition.

I would usually wake up at some point, wondering what the rooms could mean, and try to remember them exactly; looking for clues to my own state of mind in them. I was just about to open one of these doors when I was awoken by Susan.

She was shaking me by the shoulder. “Wake up Alice! I can see a light in the big house.”

Chapter Eleven
Voodoo Child

I threw myself out of bed and looked out of the rear window, facing the big house; I couldn't see a light.

"Just wait," Susan whispered. "It will be back; keep looking at the first floor."

We stood staring for some time, until there it was; the light from a torch moving along behind the fourth window, and then it was gone; appearing again in the third window, scanning up and down, as if the person holding it was looking for something.

"It could be a security guard, checking on the property," I suggested.

"Then where is their car?" I couldn't argue with that, as it seemed unlikely that they would have walked here.

"What should we do now? Do you think we should go and take a look?" I wasn't sure if I liked the sound of my own idea.

"From here we would see if they leave from the side or front. Are there any other doors? I don't remember any."

"There is another one at the back, but that had a metal security cover over it." I wracked my brain for other exits.

"Well, we probably stand more chance of seeing them from here; unless they get out through a window round the right side or the rear."

We kept watch for a couple of hours. There were no more lights, and no one left the building that we could see, so we went back to bed.

"You were right about our things being moved," I decided that I might as well tell Susan this, given the latest developments.

"And you chose to tell me this now! Well, thanks for that," she replied, grabbing a pillow and climbing into bed.

"You're welcome," I added, as we then looked uneasily about the darkened room, as I sat on the end of the bed, recalling the dip in my parents' one.

"There's a bolt on this door," I said, remembering this, "I think I'll shut it." I enjoyed the feel of the antique metal in my hand, it was as old as the wood itself, and I thought about the others who had held its weight.

"What do you think Larry meant about the locals thinking the stuff at The Inn was all down to you and your brother being there?"

"I don't know, but I don't see how it could have been, as so much of it involved my parents, and there was the bar furniture being moved; I don't see what we could have had to do with that. Not forgetting the stones coming off the walls. Perhaps they think spirits hang around children; I've heard that one before.

"I wonder what the picture was that you drew; the one the nuns gave to the priest?" I could see she had been paying attention.

"I have thought about that and I just don't get it. Surely, I would remember this. I think I'm going to have to ask my parents about it, but they won't like it, and I don't know if they'll actually tell me anything."

Another storm was starting to blow. Heavy rain pulsed in rhythmic sheets against the windows, forced on by an angry wind.

The bed was very comfortable; the mass of the duvet provided protection from the actual tempest, and the one brewing in my brain. As my head searched the sturdy pillow, I had brought it with me, for fragments of the dream I had so recently left, I couldn't discern if some of the sounds I heard came from outside or within but chose to ignore this possibility. I'd had enough for one day and closed my eyes and ears to it all.

I woke to the sound of Susan's snoring, the gale had passed and morning was fighting its way through the damask curtains. Looking around the room, I noticed that the drawers were all open and the chair was on its side. I had a flashback to the night when the roof came in on the chalet. That too had been caused by a storm, but this was different; the gatehouse was a strong building, and someone or something had been in this room, whilst we were asleep.

Or had they? The door was bolted. Concerned that my sleep walking habit may have returned, and still mulling over my part in past events, I closed the drawers and returned the chair to its former place.

I drew back the curtains, surveying The Inn and the big house; they were, certainly, spooky looking places. I didn't doubt that they could have created mysteries and suspicions in the minds of small children. But if this encouraged mischief, I couldn't say, and my brother was always taciturn on the whole subject. It seemed cruel that the locals could have blamed us for anything that went on there, and I couldn't see what it had to do with them anyway.

There was also the visit by the paranormal investigators. I wondered how they enjoyed their stay in the gatehouse. There can't have been that many of them around in the sixties, perhaps they could even still be alive, or someone might have kept their records. I found this an interesting, yet unlikely, possibility.

Then what about Judith Cunningham; why was she looking at apartments in the big house? I thought this could have been in order to be nearer to her mother; now, she definitely knew some details. Was she one of the locals pointing the finger at me?

I suddenly felt the need to get back inside the big house, and to have a look at the tenant's accommodation at The Inn. Yet, both of these were likely to be difficult to achieve. There was also 'The Circle'; I felt certain there was more to learn there. I knew it was time to enter the dark side of this place.

"Wake up, Susan; we have a lot to do today."

"Oh God, that was a horrible night's sleep," she yawned, then rolled over and closed her eyes again, but continued. "I was dreaming about the journey to the beach, the big house never seemed to get any further away, however much we walked. And, all the people from the past few days kept popping up, including that nasty old man with the fox's head; he seemed to be following us."

"Too much cheese and not enough sleep, I'd say."

"I wonder how we can find out who was in the big house last night?" she thought for a moment. "Perhaps we should ask Don and Rachel."

"I'm not sure about that, we could take a walk to the camp site and fish around, I suppose." I tried to think of a sensible plan;

fitting in as much as possible. "It would probably be a good idea to call in on Don and Rachel, to see how they're getting on with their campers, and then the rest of the day is ours for exploring. What do you think?"

"Suits me; I'm just coming along for the ride. This little break is becoming far more interesting than I ever expected it to!"

I was increasingly grateful for her company. Without Susan I wouldn't have had access to the gatehouse, or a sensible outsider to measure my behaviour by. If I was sleep walking again, she would surely spot this at some point; and if I wasn't, at least I wasn't alone.

We had our breakfast sitting in the little garden of the gatehouse and watched Larry checking The Inn garden for the day ahead.

I stood up and waved. As he headed over, I decided to cut to the chase.

"Good morning, Landlord Larry!" I took a cheerful approach, putting aside his suspicions about me and my brother.

"Good morning, ladies," he looked happy to see us.

"I hope you won't mind my asking this, Larry," I said, worried that a refusal would remove one important avenue of research from my list, "I'm feeling quite nostalgic and, dare I say, a bit home sick. I wondered if there was any way I could have a look at where I used to live; at some point convenient to you, of course?"

"I don't see why not; you'll find thing have changed though, I'm sure." I couldn't believe he'd agreed so easily and was quite speechless at his acceptance of my request. "Pop in for a drink at about nine; we only have a few regulars in after this time."

"It's a date!" I cringed at myself for putting it like this. Susan raised her eyebrows at me, again, and grinned.

When he was at a safe distance she added, "Well, that's one way to get your pub back."

"I don't know what you mean; I only want to have a look upstairs."

"And he's more than willing to show you!" she replied, rolling her eyes.

"Have you looked at my face lately?" I snorted. "I'm a bruised and invisible, over fifties rucksack carrier."

"You might not be to him," Susan said, shaking her head. "You could be a very interesting commodity."

"I don't know what you mean," I said again; I didn't, really.

"Look at this place," she waved an arm around The Inn and its garden. "It's quite dead; only regulars in after nine. What was it like when you lived here?"

Susan did have a point. It was so busy then; people came from far and wide. Even after we left, my dad had a bonus payment from the brewery for selling more of their beers than any other pub in the whole county during our tenancy. The pub business had dwindled over time, but surely not in tourist areas like this.

"It's ten o'clock; before we go to the campsite I want to go to 'The Circle', they should be open by now."

We made our way in silence across the road. I stopped before the doorway and tried to recall its former existence. Looking at the parade, I believed that it had been a sweet shop, and could see why it had changed hands; not enough money these days from selling pink shrimps and blackjacks to pay the rent.

Yet edibles, I remembered, hadn't been their only merchandise. Looking at the Victorian windowed frontage of curved glass, and carved wood, I could picture the orange cellophane that used to protect the items for sale from the ravages of the sun. There had been artist's equipment, children's pencil cases, balls and a few toys. What I remembered most were the brown school satchels; I could see my nana and grandad buying me one of these.

At the memory of this, I confidently blew past the chime of the door and made my way to the counter; where, again, the couple had their heads down in the newspaper.

"I would like a reading," I announced to anyone who would care to listen, and caught Susan baulking at the idea of this, from the corner of my eye.

"Palm or cards?" the henna haired lady asked without looking up.

"Whatever," I replied.

She lifted her head, and on seeing who it was, gave me a penetrating look. "The ball, I think, would be most suitable," her voice, however, showed no surprise at my presence.

The tie-dyed shirt and embroidered jacket were gone. Today she was decked out in full witchy wear; I wondered if this wasn't due to the visitors in the village. Her hair was now a deep, wine-red and she wore a scarlet, satin dress coat with a black laced bodice peeping out beneath it. Her cleavage had seen better days. From her neck hung a filigree, pentagram charm decorated with purple jewels, and her painted finger nails drew the eye towards the many silver rings encircling her short but dainty fingers. I also noticed that she wore a support strap on her left wrist; she was no spring chicken and probably had some aches and pains.

"If you would like to follow me to the reading room, where we will not be disturbed?"

"Is it alright if my friend comes along? I'm sure I will forget everything; I have a terrible memory."

"As you wish," on saying this, she rose from behind the counter, beckoning us towards the synthetic satin, purple curtain next to it; drawing this back to reveal a door, which she opened with a long key, attached to a chain which hung around her tiny waist.

This had probably been the stock room to the original shop. I imagined boxes of crisps and bubble gum, and the jars of many varieties of boiled sweets, neatly arranged on dark wooden shelves; which I felt sure, had lined the tiny room for many years. I could almost smell the lingering confusion of confections.

Apart from the small light cast by the barred window, which was covered with a length of creamy muslin, the room was in darkness. She drew a match from an embossed silver case to light the candle placed at the centre of the round table, which stood beneath a shroud of black cloth.

"If you would like to go over there," dispatching Susan to a wooden stool in one corner. "Now we shall take our places," she said, seating me with my back to the door; I have never liked being in this position.

Lowering herself into a throne like chair, she carefully arranged the long garments beneath her, and then gathered up a deck of tarot cards that were spread out on the table, putting them to one side. "And so we begin the cleansing ceremony," after lifting the candle and moving it in the direction of the four corners of the room, she placed it back on the cloth, before drawing her hands around the outline of my face and shoulders several times.

She then swept away a black silk scarf, in a theatrical motion, revealing the ball, "Relax and un-focus your eyes; look into the sphere and think of your question."

Who was the Night Walker and where do you fit into all of this? I thought, trying not to move my lips. I considered that it was significant that she had chosen the ball; if I knew anything about palm or card readings she wouldn't have been able to lie. Using this method, she would be able to tell me anything she wanted to; or not.

Running the lengths of her hair between her bejewelled fingers, she considered the globe in the candle light.

"Do you see?" she asked in a breathy, childlike voice.

"Not exactly," I replied, as I could see nothing.

"I see you returning to yourself."

"I have come back here."

"You are seeking for old truths, and you may not find them. There is danger in the steps you take."

"What kind of danger?" Was this a threat? I wondered how she could benefit by winding me up.

"I see a thickening mist. Ghosts walk with you," she looked pleadingly at me, and then turned to Susan, trying to reinforce this sentiment, "whilst ever you stay in this place."

"Do you see any images in the ball, beyond the mist?" I asked, feeling uncomfortable and amused at the same time.

"I see you, standing alone in darkness," she gasped.

"Well, that's unlikely, as I've hardly spent a moment alone for days."

"It could indicate a mental state of darkness; yet my senses see you in physical solitude."

This was all too serious yet hilarious at the same time; I decided to play a game. "I see you."

"Where can you see me?" she asked, surprised by this ambush.

"I see you outside The Inn," I said, in an attempt at an ethereal voice.

"I can see that my presence here, opposite The Inn, is blurring your vision. There is little point in continuing this gazing." She stood up, "Given your past, it is clear you have some sensitivity. I feel you should have a teller who is not from around here, if you should choose to take another look into the ball."

She ushered us through the door and back into the shop.

"How much will that be?" I asked, taking the purse from my rucksack.

"There will be no charge; as it was a failed reading." At this, we withdrew from 'The Circle' with a tinkle of the bell.

"What did you make of that?" I asked Susan, trying not to look back.

"Someone with something to hide, I think," she said, glancing over her shoulder.

"That's just what I thought," I replied, feeling pleased with how the day was going.

We headed off down Cart Lane, towards the camp site. "Do you have a decent phone? Mine's not so good when I want to look at things on the internet."

"Mine isn't that bad but my laptop is back at the gate house, if that could be any use?"

"Excellent. Perhaps we can connect to the wifi from The Inn later; if they have it." I had a few things I needed to look up and wanted to avoid another lengthy trip to the library in Cromer.

Chapter Twelve

Mama told me not to come

When we reached the camp site Rachel was in the field, at the back, clearing up debris from the activity of the previous night. It looked like there had been quite a party; spent candles, wine and beer bottles littered the place.

"Wow! That was some witch gathering," I exclaimed, taken aback at the unexpected state of the place, as we approached her.

"It's not normally like this; they're usually such a quiet bunch," she replied, looking like she'd had something of a night herself. "Loads of them appeared, more than those booked in. It was like a festival."

"We'll give you a hand, won't we Susan?"

Before long we had returned the field to its former state; I was eager to get Rachel back to the bungalow for a chat.

"I think you've earned yourselves a bit of a meal," she took out a walkie-talkie. "Come in Don, it's time for lunch. The girls are here."

"Coming right at you, Rachel, my luv," his voice crackled over the air waves. "I'll be there in a jiffy."

Back in the bungalow, we helped Rachel chop and prepare a splendid lunch of feta cheese, salad with olives, peppers, gherkins and couscous, and home made bread. "I don't like the big supermarket, but I have to say we didn't have much of this stuff before."

"I do know what you mean," I considered my reply. "Although, I'm sure people ate before its arrival."

"Yes, there might not have been the variety, but more locals had work," she took a deep breath.

"It must be hard round here, for everyone to find jobs; without so much farming now," Susan added, thoughtfully.

"That's been the case for a very long time," Rachel said, looking sadly into the bowl of food she was tossing vigorously. "I don't know how some people manage."

Don burst in at this point waving a pair of red knickers about his head, in a rubber gloved hand. "Well, some old bird must be feelin' a draught today!"

"Good Lord Donald! You get rid of those, right now," Rachel cried, looking very embarrassed.

"Just as you ask, my darling," he stepped back and neatly arranged the item of underwear on a trimmed box hedge, just outside the front door. "There, let that be a sign to them," he laughed, and so did we.

"What do you make of them all, Don?" The unusual activity of the Witches of Waltham began to interest me greatly.

"It's not like the normal. They have their walks; their turning about the trees, and camp fires, but last night was something else," he looked quite cross, which I had never seen so far. "They shouldn't have done it. There was about sixty of them," he said, angrily, "and they were only booked in for twenty. Mind you, none of them actually stayed here the night."

"What?" Susan asked. "None of them slept here?" looking my way, expecting me to know what she was thinking.

"No, and they haven't been back since. Just made a ruddy great mess, they did."

"Anyway, how was your night at the gatehouse?" Rachel asked, with an impish smile. "Did things go bump in the night?"

"No," I jumped in, before Susan could. "A quiet night was had by all. I didn't realise that you and Don owned the place. You've renovated it so beautifully; it's nothing like I remembered it."

"We are very pleased with it. My father bought it from Mrs Napper soon after you left; she needed an income and he'd already bought the little butler's apartment. You already recalled that I lived there."

"Is that going to be part of the new development?" Susan asked.

"We've asked the estate company to include it for the moment, and see what offers we get, but aren't sure if we'll accept. It's just sat there for years doing nothing," Don replied, looking a bit sad about this.

"Are you attached to the place, Don?" I hadn't really thought about it before but when I did, he struck me as the sentimental type.

"You're not wrong there, my luv," he sighed. It seemed I wasn't the only one with a penchant for the past. "We had some grand times there, when we were starting out together; me and Rachel. We held some lovely parties there but this was after you'd all gone to London. We even had a few of the musicians from the venue staying with us. You wouldn't believe it if I told you who."

"Yes," Rachel joined in, "we lived there happily until my parents passed away. Some twenty years, it would have been."

"When did Mrs Napper die?"

"Die? Mrs Napper?" Don laughed.

"She isn't dead Alice. She lives at a nursing home in the village now; she's a hundred and two years old."

"That's amazing!" I could hardly believe my ears. "I always thought she was ancient nearly fifty years ago."

"It was probably because of the chair and the sticks. You were so young then, anyone over forty probably looked past their sell-by date; you'd have been measuring us up for a matching pair of boxes if we looked like this back then," Rachel and Don were both equally amused by her witty response.

"Neither of you look a day over forty now, do they Susan?"

"I don't know about that," Don laughed. "Any way, how are you youngsters going to spend the rest of this fine day? A walk round the local shops?"

"We've already done that. I was going to mention, we popped into 'The Circle' this morning."

"What on earth for Alice?" Rachel said, looking surprised at this revelation.

"You don't want to be going in there," added Don, shaking his head.

"I had a crystal ball reading; I thought I'd get into the spirit of things."

"And did you notice anything about the woman proprietor?" Rachel enquired.

"No, except that she was rather done up today, but I thought that was to do with all the visitors she might be expecting."

"Anything physical; did anything stand out to you about her person?" Rachel asked, tipping her head to one side.

"Apart from her cleavage being made a bit of a feature, I did notice that she was wearing a support bandage," I didn't see how this could be relevant.

"Come over here and take a long look at this photo," Don walked us over, towards the wall, behind the juke box.

"Do you remember this one?" he asked. It was one of the professional photos of the hotpants competition.

I did. "Oh look, there's my Aunty Jane, she knew she couldn't win; no nepotism allowed."

"Yes, I remember her; nice girl. Now you look closer, do you recognise anyone else?"

I scanned the line of the variously styled hotpanted young women. The photo was a bit faded but I could still discern the dimpled PVC, velvet, and crimplene worn by most of the contestants. One girl did catch my eye; she wore a shiny pink pair. Her face was familiar. The bee sting girl, as I had called her; or the victim of the whispering in the toilet.

"Have you spotted someone?" Rachel asked.

"Yes, that's the girl who went crazy."

"And that's also the old bird with 'The Circle'. Hence, the wrist support; she still claims to have trouble with it, even after all these years." She continued, "Didn't your dad tell you to watch out for the locals?"

"You've spoken to him?"

"Of course I have, once we knew it was you, it would have been rude not to. We've always kept in touch; Christmas cards and stuff."

I felt about six years old again. I was sure they'd had a jolly old chat.

"Don't worry, it was just a friendly call," Rachel insisted, seeing my alarmed expression. "We were going to wait until you were back here to call, but he's the impatient sort."

"I suppose I am that," Don agreed.

"Well it's nice to know you're still friends after all these years," I said, not entirely convinced at the implied innocent nature of their conversation.

I thought for a moment about how any of this could be helpful to my investigation. "I know Susan would love to see inside the butler's apartment. Wouldn't you?"

"Oh yes, I'm fascinated by it all," she did look very keen on the idea.

"Is there any chance you could lend us a key, to have a little look? That's unless either of you might have the time to show us around."

"Well, I don't see what harm that could do," Don didn't seem to mind. "What do you think, Rachel?"

"I don't see why not," going over to a small table, by the front door, opening its drawer taking out a bunch of keys. "Admission to the castle!" she said, temptingly, jangling them in the air.

I couldn't believe it; keys to at least part of it, and a potential visit to my old home behind the bar, all in one day. This was progress.

"Rachel," I asked, taking possession of the keys, "who are the locals my dad said I should watch out for?"

"Us, you twit," Don grinned. "He was joking.

We all enjoyed our lunch, and had a great time revelling in some of mine and Susan's recent exploits; the ones we chose to share, at any rate.

Rachel said she had always thought Gail, the girl of the screaming and whispering, had been inspired, or scared by, an episode in the 'Randall and Hopkirk (Deceased)' television series; 'The House on Haunted Hill'. With this stimulation, Rachel believed she had begun looking for spooky stuff, and become frenzied by this; enough for her to create a scene, and lead her to starting 'The Circle'.

I could imagine how this would have been possible, in such a still and ancient place. The village must have been a real backwater then. It hadn't changed much; I was frenzied by just being there.

"She started off at first doing stalls by the beach, with stuff she ordered from London. There were always witchy folk visiting here anyway, because of the history; remember, I told you they had been coming for a long time," Don said, putting on his boots.

"What history?" Susan asked.

"I don't really know, but there are lots of marks around here-by, warding them off."

"Yes, of course, Alice pointed one of them out in the bedroom of the gatehouse."

"Poor Gail thinks she is one of them, but she's not," Rachel added.

"How do you mean?" I asked.

"Well, from what I know, they're all of old families from around here, and she doesn't belong to one; most of those Witches of Waltham are local by heritage. Her mum brought her here when she was about the age you were, when you first arrived," Rachel looked as though something had occurred to her as she said this.

"What about the old boy who runs it with her? Is he her husband?"

"Oh Lord, no," Don laughed. "She doesn't go in for them, from what I understand. He just drifted down here years ago and never left."

"Now Don, there was a man once, and you know it," Rachel said, giving him a disapproving look. "He wasn't the best of sorts, and it was a good job for her that it did come to an end."

"Yes, he's a bad sort alright," nodded Don.

"Well, this is all very mysterious," Susan interjected.

"Yes, it is," added Rachel, "and that's the way it's staying, you two. Some things are better left in the past. There's stuff best left alone."

"Now, you enjoy your snoopin'; we've got a load of messy witches to knock into shape," Don waved his hands in a spell casting gesture.

"We'll report back tomorrow," I felt the urge to give them each a hug; so I did; as did Susan.

"You do that," Rachel said, looking motherly. "Come and see us tomorrow."

Chapter Thirteen
Going in Circles

"I suggest a look round the butler's apartment, a bit of research on your laptop, and then a tour with Larry upstairs at The Inn; no jokes please."

"That sounds like an excellent plan," Susan agreed, as we walked back down Cart Lane, in the direction of the village.

I felt the power of the keys in my pocket, as we marched, purposefully, through the car park; I believed they could unlock more than doors. They offered a way to unleash my hidden memories. My visit the other day, to the big house, had just wetted my appetite; without all the other people around, I felt I could submerge myself in it, and see what this could produce.

This time, at the walled entrance to the Butler's apartment, the padlock fell open with a gratifying silence with a turn of the key. This was swiftly followed by the pleasing sound of the old bell jingling our honest arrival, as I opened the gate; this gate with its bell and the metal turn style meant something to me, but I couldn't remember what. Once in the small yard, I noticed a couple of wine bottles with the burnt out stubs of candles in their necks, and was sure they hadn't been there the day before and then, peering through a window to the butler's apartment, I could make out something drawn on the slate floor-tiles with chalk; it was a pentagram. I would certainly have noticed this before. Someone had been here since the viewing.

Upon entering, we looked in on the few small rooms, which meant nothing much to me, and then headed along the narrow corridor and climbed, cautiously, up the staircase leading into the big house.

I tried several of the keys until one fitted the lock. It clicked open but something on the other side of the door pushed against it, something refusing our entry. "It's bolted," I said, frustrated at this.

"Do you think someone knew we were coming, and has something to hide?" Susan suggested.

"You could be right." Not wanting to fall into the over superstitious trap of Gail, I added, "But, perhaps a security guard has closed the main building off."

"We're just wasting our time here now. Let's go to The Inn and ask Larry if we can use their internet access."

"Good idea, I feel that we're working against the clock for some reason."

Stepping carefully around the pentagram, not wishing to fall into its spell, we made our way out, locked the door and then padlocked the gate.

"I wonder what these other keys are for; some of them look very old." I examined the strange collection hanging from an aged RAC key ring. "Anyway, enough of this for now; there's nothing more for us here."

Seen from the front of the big house, The Inn, and the gatehouse, looked perfectly harmless on that early summer's evening. It was hard to imagine the dangerous smuggling activities, that had helped the locals survive; or not, in some cases.

Witches and ghosts were also absent from this pleasant village setting; yet we knew they had run amok.

I tried to picture dark nights, when they had moved, secretly, around this space; conjuring up images of their exploits. Shady figures in tricorn hats, cloaked coats and long tan boots came out at me from the brick work. Many muffled conversations and curses were surely heard from dim corners around here; arguments perhaps. Apart from the smugglers, whose business it was easier to imagine, I wondered why the witches were drawn to The Inn; then and now.

We went back to the gatehouse and loafed around for a while. I said I needed forty winks and climbed the stairs to the bedroom. I considered the drawers and the chair; wondering why and how I could have disturbed them in such a way during the previous night, without Susan waking up, and surveyed the room for any other possible access. Going back to my days with the Doctor, I felt along the wooden panelling and around the fire place, without any luck.

I shook off my boots and rested on the bed, in an attempt to recreate my former slumber. Drifting in and out of a nap, my brain tried to tell me something that was just without my grasp. It involved a previous visit to the gatehouse, one somewhere deep in my memory. I was sitting on the floor; there were lots of long legs in jeans, stretching out, and sunlight from the window to The Inn garden played across canvas rucksacks. It wasn't a bad memory at all, if anything, I knew I had been happy down there.

Rousing myself, I saw that it was six o'clock and decided that this would be a good time to ask Larry about the possibility of using the wifi connection from The Inn. There were three useful hours before our potential visit to the licences' accommodation and I wanted to make the most of these; we had nothing else to do.

I went into the bathroom and looked at myself in the mirror, which I hadn't done all day. Still quite a sight, I took a shower, tried to make myself as presentable as I could, and went downstairs.

"That's better," Susan said, looking unashamedly relieved; I knew I had let things slide a little. "My turn now, give me twenty minutes."

I made a list of the things I wanted to look up on the internet. We needed to search for anything to do with Mrs Napper; find out the real name of the big house; all local deaths in nineteen seventy - plus finding out about any witchy activity and incidents of haunting in the area. I put it in my pocket just as Susan appeared. She looked very attractive in her t-shirt, jeans and tasselled loafers. If Larry was interested in a new female friend, I felt certain that she would have been above me on the menu; the dish of the day.

We went through the side-gate that led directly onto the lawn of The Inn. A few families and pairs relaxed at tables, but most of them were still empty. I liked passing through the heavy, round-topped door, tucked behind two pillars that supported the tilted tiled roof, which had remained as it was in my memory. In summer months it had previously been kept open with an elaborate iron shoe scraper, which stood on a heavy stone base. I thought it would have been more welcoming to customers if Larry still kept it open in some way, but was glad to feel the lift of the old latch all the same.

The stone floor of the saloon, no doubt originating from its former life as stables, had been covered with a large, red and green patterned rug when we lived there; I remembered all the hoovering. I was glad to see this had been revealed, I hadn't notice this change before but it gave an authentic feel to the old place.

It was very quiet in there, with no music and just a smattering of drinkers dotted about.

"Why now, am I glad to see you two?" Larry called from behind the bar.

"It's nice to see you as well, Larry," I replied, surprised at such an enthusiastic welcome.

"Now then girls, it's going to be a busy night and I've got no barmaid; bless her, she's called in sick. What do you say? Are you up for it?"

"I'm sure we'll do anything we can to help, won't we Susan?"

"Of course, I'd be only too glad to," she looked a little bemused by the situation.

"Why we came over so early, though, was to ask if we could use your wifi in the gatehouse, if it will work over there.

"That's not a problem; I'll give you the code right now."

"And as it's so quiet in here at the moment, I hope you won't mind if Susan leaves us for an hour or so, to look up a few things; we're hoping to visit a few places further afield in the next few days. We need to plan our journeys carefully, as we don't drive."

"Splendid idea, I'm glad to see that you're making the most of Norfolk."

I took out my list and wrote the wifi address on the back of it; handed it to Susan, flipping it over to show her what I wanted her to look into.

As Susan went out two young women came in, closely followed by a young man with a beard.

"You made it then," Larry said to them. "If you'd like to sort yourselves out in the corner, over there, I'll get the extension lead out."

The women wore long dresses, one in cornflower blue and the other in white. The young man was carrying a guitar, and then another one clattered in; a slightly older man, with a keyboard in a hard case.

As they set up, other customers arrived including Judith Cunningham, and an elderly lady, who I assumed to be her mother.

They came over to me, as I stood, feeling slightly smug, behind the bar.

"I see you're in your rightful place," Judith sniped.

"Yes, it's good to be back," I felt around for a suitable response. "What's your pleasure?" I asked, doubting that she would request the pond water I wanted to serve her.

"Two small glasses of white wine please, Alice."

The old lady followed me around the bar with her eyes, as I sought out an opened bottle in the fridge.

The till was electronic and simple to use, I just tapped the image for the items and finished the transaction. There used to be just an old fashioned till, that didn't do many, if any, of the calculations for you; I had often marvelled at the skills of my parents and others counting back the change.

"I hope you're enjoying your stay?" the old lady asked, politely enough.

"Yes, thank you. It would be nice to have a chat with you later, if we're not too busy."

"It looks as though you will be kept behind there," Judith nodded towards the door, through which a large crowd of the witchy crew were entering.

I remembered Don saying that there had been about sixty of them, at the camp site, and it seemed all of them had headed to The Inn that night. I certainly had my work cut out for me behind the bar and was glad of the modern technology; my mental arithmetic couldn't have kept up with the sales.

The band were, surprisingly, good; although I wondered how they would have faired in the, now seemingly defunct, auditorium, at the rear of The Inn. I couldn't imagine how my parents ever managed to draw enough people here to fill the huge place.

As it was, the group played mostly traditional folk music and a few cover versions of pop songs from the sixties and seventies; political and sentimental. The girls had well trained and beautiful voices. They were singing 'Big Yellow Taxi' as Susan re-entered the bar.

"I've found something," she whispered to me between customers. "It's from the National Archives; a small newspaper report of a local man, missing, presumed drowned."

"We'll have to talk later, when it isn't so busy," I said, frustrated at this.

"I'll come and help you," she said, lifting the hatch.

We were kept on our toes until shortly after the band stopped playing. I wanted to speak to Judith, and her mum, before they left. I had to find out about the picture I had drawn, knowing I couldn't research that one on the internet.

I went over, bearing two more glasses of white wine. "Judith, did you enjoy the band?" I asked cheerfully, like she was the friend she hadn't been.

"Oh yes, it's always good to hear them play. My daughter, Agnes, is the one in the blue dress." I was shocked that she could have produced such splendid offspring.

"You must be so proud; what a lovely voice she has," I added, genuinely.

"Mother, you remember Alice?" Judith said, smiling at me, almost apologetically for having to remind her mother who I was.

Her mother was well into her eighties, I thought she was doing well keeping up with the evening.

"I do remember you, how could I forget?"

"Forgive me for seeming surprised, but I don't see that I could have made such a great impression."

"You, and your brother, were always up to mischief."

"Were we? I can't say that I remember." I was quite shocked at this.

"You drew that horrid picture of Mr Napper; right there behind the bar, where he died. Looking all ghoulish and boggle eyed at the stabbing"

"But I can't have; I don't even know what Mr Napper looked like." I was only six-years-old for goodness sake! Where would I have seen a picture of Mr Napper, and how would I have known about 'the stabbing'? I wondered if Mrs Napper hadn't told or shown me something.

I hadn't noticed Susan, clearing glasses from the table behind us, until she spoke. "Did you actually see the drawing?"

"What's that to you?" the old lady asked in a rough tone.

"She's Alice's friend, Mother," Judith interjected, with a knowing look.

"Oh, you are, are you now? Well, your friend was always up to no good."

"What? At six years old?" Susan responded, indignantly.

"Mrs Cunningham, I'm only trying to piece the facts together. I hope it won't be too much of an imposition to ask you to share what you do know?" I asked, as gently as I could.

"Things were always quiet round here, before your lot turned up."

"My lot, I don't know what you mean?" I was becoming increasingly confused.

"You and your family," she added, looking very disgruntled. "We didn't need livening up."

"Surely, The Inn doing well meant more work for locals?" Susan said, also becoming confused by this attack.

"Your lot started something, and it lasted for years after you went on your merry way."

"Come on Mother," Judith threw herself into the fray. "We've had enough of this nonsense now."

And off they went.

"Well, that was interesting," Susan said, shaking her head in disbelief.

"Yes, what a pair," something occurred to me. "Do you know, the girl in the blue dress is Judith's daughter but I didn't see them speak to her once, unless I was too busy to notice?"

"They certainly don't think much of you, or your family."

"The feeling is mutual, at least on my part, and I don't know what she could mean about 'it' lasting for years."

Chapter Fourteen
Spill the Wine

A young man had appeared behind the bar by the time we got back there and Larry came over.

"Thanks for your help girls, it's much appreciated. Rob here can take over now. I suppose you'll want to have that look behind and upstairs; you've certainly earned it."

He then lifted the hatch of the bar, allowing our entry behind there again and beckoned us; pointing to a door I was very familiar with.

"Aren't you coming Larry?" Susan asked.

"Oh no, I don't believe you'll need a commentary from me interrupting Alice's memories."

"This is very kind of you, Larry," I said, surprised that we were going to wander around his home unsupervised.

The door opened to a small hallway, with a clear view into the downstairs quarters, and a flight of dark wooden stairs.

Susan appeared animated by the options, "Which way first, Alice?"

"It has to be up!" I had no doubt about that; I wanted as much time as we could get in the bed rooms.

The stairs themselves were as I remembered, despite the dull patterned runner that I could picture being now gone. The walls had since been decked out with photos of bands that had, I assumed, played at the venue behind The Inn; some of them were instantly recognisable.

"Well, I can see that they were busy here after we left."

"Is that…" Susan exclaimed, pointing to a black and white photo of a riotous punk band thrashing away.

"I believe it is."

On reaching the landing, I half expected to have to step over Bobby; keeping his loyal guard between us and below. Whilst regretting his absence, I noticed something still present; the sun-bleached painting of The Night Walker.

"Look at this Susan!" I called out, hardly believing my eyes. "It's my phantom."

We peered studiously at the dirty old painting. The name of the artist was a scratchy blur but a plaque at the foot of the frame named the 'sitter', although he was, in fact, standing; it read, Cornelius Walker.

"Well, there's one mystery solved," I sighed, as this success mingled with the feeling of disappointment at it all being so simply explained. "There's our Night Walker."

I had the vague recollection that our games of Tardis expeditions had been an attempt to revisit the eighteenth century, in order to defeat this time traveller. He certainly was an unpleasant looking character; I couldn't imagine why he had been allowed to hang around here for so many years.

Thinking again that he must have been a significant local, and of some importance to this place, I looked, not at him but at the surrounding land, and out into the dark horizon. Again, I tried to dismantle the buildings around here, and not just the recent ones this time. I had a strong feeling that the field was somewhere on the footing of The Inn and the big house; it had to be. There was more to this, and the other painting, than met the eye; they were symbolic of Cornelius Walker's existence in this place. I felt that he still had a presence here; not, necessarily, in the bumps in the night way.

"He's an odd looking buzzard," Susan said, after gazing on him for the time my attention had been elsewhere. "That scythe looks more like a threat than a farmer's tool, and look at the way his eyes have been painted," we both moved in closer, seeking them out beneath the deep brim of his hat. "Unless he had some sort of condition, it seems to be making the point that he can see in all directions; I think it's quite deliberate," and, taking out her phone, she took a photo.

"Good idea, we'll have to see if we can't get one, of the other portrait, in the big house, and then we can compare them."

We had spent more time looking at this than I anticipated, although it was no doubt useful, I was worried about how long Larry would leave us up there. "We'd better get a move on."

My parents' former bedroom was now Larry's domain. Gone was the dark wardrobe, with matching drawers and dressing table; still very much used in London. The small double bed, covered with a cream duvet, pine chest of drawers and wardrobe made the room look lighter than it had done in the past.

The wood of the panelling had been taken back to its natural colour and was treated with a protective wax finish. I felt along this for secret entrances but knew that I would be unlikely to find any after the refurbishment, and the original carpenters were, no doubt, very clever. The floor boards, renovated by the same method, were flawless; I couldn't discern any of our spy holes.

In my old room, there was nothing more than a single bed and canvas wardrobe, which was empty. I ran my hand along the mantle piece of the brick work fire place, trying to take myself back. I looked at the diamond shaped leaded windows, they followed a pattern; repeated in all those throughout the building. The colours worked in diagonal lines of four blue, with four clear following behind; on the line below there were dull amber, green or violet glasses breaking up this sequence. There was something different about the last of the three panes, making up the casement window to my old bedroom; something odd about the top corner on the left. I opened the middle section, the only one with an armed hinge, and stuck my head out. "Give me your phone, Susan." I leant out and took a photo. When we looked at it, we were shocked to see the image of a man, wearing a hat, with an open, grinning mouth.

"What the hell does that mean?" Susan asked.

"Your guess is as good as mine!"

I then noticed that the inside ledge was proud of the wall, which didn't make sense, as it wasn't made into a window seat; it was just a ridiculously wide sill.

"Where are my excellent barmaids? Larry's voice travelled up the stairs. "It's getting very busy down here girls."

"We're coming, Larry," I rolled my eyes at Susan. "Well, that's it for now."

The saloon was full of young people, and the witchy crowd; there was a noticeable air of anticipation.

"I'm sorry to interrupt you but we've certainly got our hands full here tonight."

"That's alright, Larry," Susan said. "We're only too glad to help, aren't we Alice?"

"Of course; it's great to see the old place heaving with life!"

Amidst the throng, I spotted Gail and her business partner. They appeared to be either arguing or in debate about something. She stood up and he grabbed her arm; the one with the support strap, and I saw her wince. Trying to lip read what he was saying; I thought I made out the words, 'No you don't!' I followed her eyes, they seemed drawn to that horrible man with the fox's head hanging from his belt; I hadn't noticed he was here also.

We continued collecting glasses between serving the odd drink; I thought it would be a good way to mingle, and pick up on the odd bit of conversation but we learned nothing to our advantage. Time passed very quickly, before long the bell rang for last orders, and the bar emptied soon after.

Larry asked us to stay behind for a drink, before returning to the gatehouse. He took us into the sitting room of the living quarters. "We'll be more comfortable in here," he said, plumping a cushion.

I avoided Susan's eye, knowing the look she would give me at this suggestion, not wanting Larry to read anything into it.

I gave the room a cursory inspection but was more interested in anything we could learn from Larry. "That was quite a crowd," I said, choosing a cushion-free chair.

"Yes, I haven't had such a good night here since New Year's Eve," he spoke before taking a long drink from his pint. "I could do with a few more like it. What was your dad's trick? He could draw a crowd. Gigs in the concert hall are one thing, but that depends on who you've got on; keeping The Inn going is a different matter."

"Do you run the concert hall?" Susan asked.

"No, that's a separate business now. Of course, I benefit when there's a show, but those are few and far between now. Unless they can improve the building, to meet regulations, that's going to become housing as well."

"What a shame," we said, simultaneously, including Larry.

"Larry, do you remember my little run in with Judith Cunningham the other night?"

"Oh yes, I do," he laughed.

"What do you know about her? Her mother seems very agitated about the time my family were here and something this led to."

"What else did they tell you?"

"Judith did mention that her daughter was one of the singers tonight, the girl in the blue dress."

"Did you see the girl's father here tonight?"

"No, it was just Judith, and her lovely mother," I couldn't remember seeing the man who had been with her at the big house, or on the walk, unless I had missed him.

"He was here alright," he said, taking another drink and grinning. "The dirty old devil; I bet that put her nose right out."

I found it hard to believe we were talking about the same person; this couldn't be the mild mannered man I'd seen Judith with.

"Yes, the man who time forgot," he said, standing up. "It's a long story; I'll get us another drink to wash it down with," and off he went.

When he left, I remembered that Susan was trying to tell me something earlier. "What were you going to say about the newspaper article?"

"It was disappointingly brief, dated July, nineteen seventy. Just something about a local man, unnamed, missing presumed drowned. It struck me as significant; I couldn't find anything relating to it after that though."

"I think we'll have to ask Rachel and Don about that one, unless we manage to work it out for ourselves."

Larry reappeared with the drinks. "You make yourselves comfortable; this is a rough ride," he said, lowering the tray carefully onto the table. "After you left, the place was a hive of musical activity for years; all the bands, on their way up, played at the back there. Lots of local parents didn't like it; their teenagers were running wild. One of them was Judith; Mohican hair, fishnets, and the rest. Her mum didn't know what to do with her." I thought this was hilarious. "When there were no bands around, for her to mess about with, she took up with an older man; one who already had a woman."

"Tell us more Larry, the suspense is killing me," Susan's jaw dropped further at every word he spoke.

"And what would you think if I told you that she worked for 'The Circle' when she left school? In the shop, and selling their nonsense at a stall in the foyer to the hall; she was with them for about ten years."

"Them? I thought the business was Gail's?" I asked, trying to get my facts straight.

"Old Mr Foxy was her partner in crime, and in the other sense; at least that was the case before Judith found herself with a little cub in the oven, and then he got the boot from Gail."

"No! I can hardly believe it," I was astounded. "Not the man with the fox's head on his belt?"

"What an image, I'd like to put that one back in its box," Susan said, draining her glass and sucking on an ice cube.

"It doesn't end there. Judith trotted off to London, with one of the bands, and left Grandma holding baby Agnes; but Mr Foxy wasn't having this and eventually took her off, to live in a commune he'd set up."

"Well, there's no wonder Judith whipped Grandma off as quickly as she could." I said, finishing my beer. "She wouldn't have wanted me to hear that cat being let out of the bag."

I wrote my mobile number down and gave it to Larry. "If you need our services again, feel free to call us. It's been quite an experience."

"I'm with you on that one," Susan added, looking distinctly glassy eyed; I thought he must have been giving her double measures and felt relieved that ale was my tipple. I did feel quite sloshed though.

We stumbled back to the gatehouse, chewing over the evening's events and took ourselves upstairs, with glasses of water. It had been an interesting day and I was looking forward to the dreams this might throw up. I drew the bolt and surveyed the room, hoping I wouldn't go crashing about in the night again; if I had done before. Peeping out of the rear window, overlooking the big house, all seemed quiet and I couldn't see any lights from the second floor.

Susan was already snoring, as my head hit my personal pillow. I wondered how tomorrow could possibly live up to today. This was not what I expected at all when I boarded the train a week ago. Everything outside the village seemed insignificant now. How could the superior Judith have led such a previous existence? I tried to picture her with a Mohawk but this collided with jumbled images of Mr Foxy, the two paintings of Cornelius Walker and the creepy, grinning man, decorating my old bedroom window.

I woke up with a mouth like the bottom of a parrot's cage, at some point, and drank my water; somewhere in the distance I heard the sound of laughter and screams. I didn't pay much attention to this and fell back to sleep. I didn't know how much time must have passed when a loud thud brought me out of my dreams. I sat up for ages, waiting for this to happen again but it didn't, although, with my head again on the pillow, I thought I could hear someone calling 'What the hell are you doing?' over and over again. When, I eventually managed to drag myself to the window, it was morning, and I realised that this was just a couple of magpies sitting in the trees, bickering.

Chapter Fifteen

Moondance

Adjusting myself to the new day and trying to decide what to do next, I was taken by surprise when my mobile started ringing and was even more nonplussed to hear Larry's voice; having forgotten that I'd given him my number.

"Alice, I've only been sodding burgled!"

"What? I can't believe it, how awful. Wake up Susan; sorry Larry," I replied, trying to collect myself. "Are you alright? You didn't catch them or anything?"

"No, I slept through it. I came downstairs and they've nicked all the spirits, and bottled beers," he said, sounding very distressed. "The police are on their way."

"We'll be right over."

Forgetting where I was, I had somehow expected the flashing lights of a smart squad car but instead of this a solitary, slightly worse for wear, constable was making his way up to The Inn as we headed across the lawn.

Larry opened the door in his pyjamas, "Morning Sam." He obviously knew the constable, not surprisingly, given that he did run a pub and realising there was probably only one police officer in this area.

"Morning Larry, well this is a to-do."

"That it is," Larry replied, speaking more 'local' than usual.

"Did you lock yourself in proper last night?" The constable asked, taking out his notebook.

"As usual, I checked all windows and doors before going bed."

"Good man," he said, writing something. "I must say, it was a dreadful night round here; I had to get the boys from Cromer in. I should have known something like this would have happened."

"What do you mean?" Susan asked.

"Sam, these are my friends Susan and Alice; they're staying in the gatehouse and helped me out behind the bar last night."

"And did *you* hear anything going on in the night?" he said, turning his gaze on us. I felt uncomfortable at this.

"Well, I did hear some laughing and shouting but didn't think too much of it; given that it is the holiday season and lots of young people had been in The Inn last night," this was the best I could come up with, not knowing what else I could add.

"Yes, we had a large crowd heading down to the beach at dawn; I don't think they realise how dangerous it can be. All clambering around on the rocks, as the tide was still on its way out. We had the dogs on the job and everything; bloody idiots."

"Did you pull any of them?"

"Well Larry, we have a few of them in custody for minor offences; if we find any of your bottles in their belongings, that's the best we can hope for at the moment."

"I understand, Sam; sorry you've had such a bad time of it."

There was nothing else he could do, and after a quick look around he went on his way.

"I'm so sorry, Larry," I said, feeling sad for him, after such a good night's business.

"Oh well, no one was hurt," he replied, trying to look cheerful. "I'd better sort out what I can from the cellar and call the brewery."

"We'll help," Susan said, giving me half a nod.

"Yes, no doubt about that," I agreed.

I was expecting to go down to some mysterious basement, having completely forgotten that the 'cellar' was on the ground floor, at the back of The Inn.

We helped Larry restock the bar as best we were able to, given the limited supplies, and went back to the gatehouse; after saying we would pop back later, to see how he was getting on.

At the gatehouse we did a bit of exploring on the internet, and were disappointed to find nothing about the big house; not even its name. This seemed very odd. All other large houses we found on Google Earth, and did a little bit of research on, eventually led us to some information of their histories. However, the big house was untraceable, even by post code; this seemed strange, given the prospect of the potential development. It was as though it had been hidden.

We searched the census details for decades, but when we found likely results they seemed to have too few residents for such an enormous building. We were quite baffled.

"I didn't get the chance to look up Mrs Napper last night," Susan remembered. We typed her name and location into the National Archives search engine and couldn't' find anything.

"Wait a minute, try Mrs Evelyn Napper," remembering her full name from the photograph in the library. This still brought up nothing.

"Evelyn could have been her husband's first name, it's probably too antiquated as a form of address for then, but you never know."

"Let's just try Evelyn Napper." We then struck gold. Three articles repeated over and over again in different national newspapers, about Evelyn Napper of The End House, Wythrum.

"I can see how 'The End House' would have made some sense as its title; it was the end then, before other houses were built on the road to the coast," Susan said, turning the sound of its name over in her mouth.

"I don't like 'The End House', I think it's quite horrid," I was upset at this being the name of my big house. I wanted something more elegant, or grand, for the old place.

"Yes," Susan agreed. "It isn't a fitting name; I wonder if it was just the location that led to that choice, or something else, in fact."

"It could have just been 'End House', I would have preferred that," I thought out loud. "I don't like 'The', it makes it sound sinister."

The news items were interesting. The first of these announced the post-war reopening of the big house and Inn as luxurious attractions for hunting and shooting. It seemed to be more of an advertisement than anything, giving details of the grand apartments available, the services and entertainment provided, and hire of seasoned hunter horses; or stabling, for those bringing their own mounts. This was shared in newspapers up and down the country.

The second article, of the same year, was about the withdrawal of money paid to farmers; as compensation for the hunts wrecking their land. Mr Napper was named as one of the hunt organisers in the dispute.

The third announced the mysterious stabbing of Mr Napper, in nineteen-fifty-six, at The Inn. Apparently, no one witnessed the event, and no culprit was found guilty of the offence.

"I can see how the second article might have led to the third," Susan suggested.

"Yes, that wouldn't have made him very popular round here. It does explain the size of the house; it was probably built for hunting and shooting weekends. If those walls could speak, I bet they'd have a few stories to tell!"

"They can't speak, but Mrs Napper can."

"I'm not sure about that one, Susan," I felt uneasy at the prospect of involving my, now ancient, chocolate supplier in our research.

"Well, it's a thought; it's amazing that she's still around. Why don't we ask Don and Rachel if they think we would be able to visit her?"

"Let's go and see them, we could tell them about the robbery at The Inn and go from there."

"Good idea," Susan said, snapping the laptop shut.

We headed off, back down Cart Lane; I wondered what state the back field would be in, and how Rachel and Don had got on with their witches. I stopped outside the Arts and Crafts house, trying to remember what it looked like inside. I had a vague memory of losing a tooth in there; I felt the sensation of wobbling it, and began to see a great, brick fireplace, wooden panelling, yet again, and a comfortable, sagging, red sofa. I was pleased that I had ever seen inside such a building; somehow, knowing that this had been a good place to be.

A minibus was pulling out of the campsite entrance, and I could make out some of the faces I had seen in 'The Circle' at its windows. Two old estate cars emerged after this, with a procession of New Age types following them on foot. I had the impression that the party was over.

Don was holding guard, scowling at them from the doorway of the bungalow. "Bloody, good riddance," he called out, as he saw us approaching. "I don't know if we'll have them back again," he said, shaking his head.

"What on earth has happened?" Susan asked, concerned; he was clearly, very angry.

"The police were round here this morning; never happened before. They say it's not our fault, and that some stupid thing went out on that Facebook nonsense, bringing all the others here."

"We've just left the Inn; it was broken into last night," I said, realising that he probably already knew this.

"Don't I just know it, and it was probably some of them that did it, unless I'm a complete idiot."

"It's not your fault Don," Susan tried to console him. "You can't be held responsible for everyone who stays here."

"After all the stuff they had to put up with in the village, with the bands that used to come here, I don't want it all to start again, and them pointing the finger at us this time round."

"Surely, 'The Circle' must have more to do with them being here than you do? You're just where they stay," I offered, thinking this might help.

"What, old Gail?" he replied, considering this for a moment. "No, she wouldn't like them trampling all round the place. If there's anyone local behind this, it's that ex of hers, Sam Walker."

"What?" I was shocked to hear the name. "Is Sam Walker the man with the fox's head on his belt?"

"Yes, and he's enough to put any woman off men for life, and don't you know it."

"Well, he is an unpleasant looking character," I added, not knowing what to make of this, just as Rachel appeared behind Don.

"Oh Don!" she didn't look impressed. "Come in girls; apparently Alice doesn't' remember everything, and this is best said within four walls."

I had no idea what was going on or what to expect. I could think of no connection between my younger self and Sam Walker; the creep with the creature. Rachel led us over to the picture of the Western Day.

"Have a good look, Alice," she was so serious that I felt like I was being interviewed by the police myself. "You asked about someone else in this photo before, and we lied because we didn't want to bring up bad stuff. I'm sorry."

"That man at the end, the one I said looked miserable, is that him? He looks very different," he must have been in his twenties then and looked quite normal, but there was something behind the eyes; he was scheming.

Chapter Sixteen

Evil Ways

"Sam Walker did odd shifts behind the bar, like many round here; fitting them in between other work. I couldn't really say what else he did, but he lived in a caravan at the back of the big house, when you were here," Rachel said.

"Did he have a motor bike?" I asked.

"Yes, he did," Don answered, looking stony-faced.

Things began to make sense, well, sort of, at least. My brother and I must have known or suspected something about Sam Walker, as I now realised, it was he who was the main object of our spying activities.

Rachel continued, "There had been some petty thefts from The Inn, your dad knew it was none of the others and believed Sam Walker was responsible; but he had to catch him at it."

Don took over, "That's where your uncle Jack and his friends come into this."

"I'm getting confused," I was at a loss as to what they could have had to do with this. As I have said, all our family came to visit us and seemed to be in the know about something, but I had no idea what this was. I swam around my own head, searching for the things I had heard snippets of, and had tried to piece together without the help of my brother; he would only talk about the ghostly stuff, and then, eventually, even those conversations ended. I remembered the eavesdropping, and the avoidance of the subject of the man with the motor bike.

"You remember the paranormal investigators I mentioned on the walk?" Rachel asked.

"Yes, but I'd never heard of them before."

"Well, that's because there weren't any," Rachel said, as she and Don smiled at this point.

"Now, I'm getting a bit lost here," Susan piped up from the rear.

"Sorry Susan, my luv, hold on there and all will be revealed," Don took her by the arm and looked into her eyes. "Sometimes people misunderstand things, and sometimes these misunderstandings are useful."

"Stop it Don, you'll scare the poor girl," Rachel pointed to Sam Walker. "Now, does he look a slippery fellow?"

"Yes, he does," Susan agreed.

"Alice's dad had to be even more slippery to uncover him. So, when her uncle Jack and his friends arrived, who were all students with an interest in psychology, a misunderstanding got around that they were here to investigate the happenings at The Inn. We all let them think this was true."

"He would have thought they were looking for something else, when they were really watching him?" I said, feeling my way around the possibilities of this revelation.

"Exactly," Don and Rachel said, in unison.

"But they weren't the only ones watching him," Rachel added. "Mrs Napper was also onto him. Before she was married her name was Walker, Sam is her nephew."

"I think I need to sit down," I had begun to feel quite dizzy. Again, I had the feeling that my little self had been up to something, and was overwhelmed by this. Rachel hurried off and retuned with a glass of water. I stared into it and remembered the crystal ball at 'The Circle'. I was in the throws of too much information, agitating my already stressed mind, when I pictured those corridors of rooms again and had a panic attack. I couldn't swallow and found myself pacing about. Rachel brought the glass to my mouth and told me to drink.

Then, Rachel, Don and Susan helped me into the therapy room; I felt as though I was at the centre of an exorcism of sorts. Susan and Don lit the candles, turned on the music and closed the curtains while Rachel encouraged me into a chair. Again, I felt the energy from her hands pass over me.

I don't know how much time had passed, but I eventually woke up on the sofa bed. When I returned to the sitting room, I was greeted with a concerned silence and sat down on the Chesterfield.

"Your uncle and his friends believed that because you were so young, if you didn't talk about what had happened, you would forget all about it," Rachel began.

"That's true, I don't remember, but underneath the memories I have, I know there are things I want to remember but can't. I don't remember whatever happened but even knowing there was some sort of event involving Sam Walker, I still don't think that's what I feel so upset about."

"Yes," she continued "that's mostly what they hoped for, but you, obviously, haven't really forgotten."

Don stepped in, "They realised that he was sneaking about The Inn at night, somehow. Mrs Napper knew the same, and that he was getting into the big house; even though he was her nephew, he shouldn't have been in there like that. They'd already had some sort of falling out. I think he'd been having parties and stuff in there; that's why he was in the caravan. She gave you a note, telling your dad to go and visit her to discuss it all. It was on the Western Day that he knew his game was up, and you were in the frame, or at least an opportunity for him to get some sort of revenge."

I had a flashback to sitting in the garden with our dog, Bobby, and my little plate of American fried chicken. Sam was the person who had spoken to me.

"You disappeared," Rachel seemed to be reliving the event as she said these words. "Everyone searched for you, hour after hour. We were all in a terrible state. You had just vanished."

"One of your uncle's friends found Bobby, hanging around in the courtyard, to our place in the big house, and came to get me," Don said, looking agitated. "We let Bobby inside and he led us up into the main building. Eventually he found you in one of the rooms; you were crying and staring out of the window, saying a man told you Rachel was waiting for you but that you had got lost and couldn't find her."

"All hell broke loose," Rachel said, furiously. "The next night you we took you to my parents' place, here at the camp site, and a real fuss was made of you; they had a donkey brought there and everything. After this, your brother went to stay with his friend over the road for the night and you stayed here."

"The rest of us flushed Walker out," Don said, triumphantly.

"But things didn't go quite as planned," Rachel glanced at Don as she spoke. "The men chased him down to the beach, the tide was coming in and he was gone. We all thought he was dead."

"Although this all sounds awful, I still feel there was something else."

"I don't know about that," Don said, trying not to look at Rachel. I somehow knew that they were telling me all this, to put me off the track of my latent memories. I didn't believe they were doing this to hide something they had done; more that there was something that I had been guilty of.

"Was Sam Walker the missing local man, presumed dead, in the local papers at the time?" Susan was on the ball.

"My, you have been doing your research," Don said, with his hands on his hips, shaking his head in admiration. "It was him, alright. He appeared again, soon enough, like nothing had happened; and what had happened, really? What could he be charged with? Telling Alice to go to the butler's apartment? But we knew he had done more than this, apart from the supposed thefts. He must have left you inside with the door open to the big house, knowing you might go up there, and shut you in. You wouldn't have been able to reach up to the latch on the other side; it was a very cruel thing to do," he said, looking very solemnly at me.

"But what happened after this? Susan asked.

"Nothing really," Rachel answered, looking deflated at her own response. "All I know is that he had some sort of conversation in the big house with Mrs Napper, and your dad, Alice."

"Did he leave the village?" I wondered how he could have remained, after this, but quickly remembered his involvement with Gail, and Judith Cunningham.

"He was given all sorts of jobs no one else would want to do around the place, by his aunt," Don said, looking apologetic. "He wasn't paid, had his meals with her; kept to his caravan, with his head well and truly down, or so we believed."

"What do you mean?" I asked, wondering why they thought he hadn't been playing by the rules.

"Sam Walker is a bad lot; he's always up to something and always has been. There's no way he would doff his cap and totally submit," Don said, looking at Rachel.

"I wonder?" Susan added. "Did everything go quiet at The Inn after this?"

"Well, now you ask, I'd have to say things got worse," Don appeared to be registering something that hadn't occurred to him before. "Did you used to go to the gatehouse, when you lived at the Inn?"

"Yes, sometimes, with Mrs Napper's friend; when she was getting the place ready for the next visitors."

"And did she mind the job?" Don said, looking at me, expectantly.

"I do remember us often being told to wait at the bottom of the stairs, for what seemed like a lifetime." I could still picture that child safety-gate.

"Yes, that's because she was scared out of her skin and didn't want to be alone in the place. Mrs Napper sold it to Rachel's dad, soon after you had gone, even though it was her main source of income by then."

"To be honest," Rachel said, "I don't remember if any strange stuff continued at The Inn after the business with Sam Walker, but there was a particular event at the gatehouse that led Mrs Napper to sell it."

"A group of bikers had set up camp that summer, behind the big house, I didn't know them," Don stressed, "and Sam Walker insisted he didn't either, but I wouldn't be too sure about that though. They took to riding round the place, and up and down Beach Lane, after The Inn was closed. They were only here for a few months, and it was on the last night of their antics that the couple staying at the gatehouse ran out of it in a state of horror, narrowly missing being run over by the bikes, and banged on The Inn door."

"Your dad brought them round to the butler's apartment; I looked after the lady while Don and your dad went back with the man."

"They had woken up, feeling that someone had been in the bedroom with them. The man had gone downstairs and found pentagrams painted all over the walls and floor. It was a sight; we couldn't work out how they had got in there, but with the sound of the bikes outside, after they had fallen asleep, they might not have noticed other noises."

"We found a pentagram, drawn on the floor of the kitchen, in the butler's apartment," I thought it was about time I mentioned this.

"What?" Rachel was livid. "And you didn't think to tell us?"

"We came to tell you today; you had enough on your plate with the witch brigade," I wasn't sure that we were going to reveal this, but it seemed as good a time as any; I was wrong, apparently.

"And is there anything else you two aren't telling us?" Don joined in.

"We thought we saw a light, in the big house, the other night," Susan spluttered out, nervously.

I quickly realised this wasn't my story, it was real life; it belonged to Rachel and Don. We were outsiders, and how ever much I felt part of the place, I had been a visitor, and that was all I ever would be.

"Do you have the keys?" Rachel asked, sternly.

"No, they're at the gatehouse," I answered, feeling very uncomfortable.

"Well, we'll see you there at nine tonight," she huffed.

At this we left; there was no fond farewell.

We walked in silence along Cart Lane, until we came to the green.

"Do you think we should leave?" Susan asked, seemingly growing uncomfortable with the situation.

"No, I think we should see it through," I wasn't entirely sure if this was a good idea but we had come this far.

"I hoped you'd say that, if we leave now we'll never know."

"Never know what?" I asked, grateful for her continued curiosity at events.

"What the hell is going on round here!" she stopped, raising her hands in disbelief.

"I agree, let's go back and see what's been going on at The Inn; we've got hours until they come for the keys," I replied, secretly wanting to get back upstairs and have a look at the little passage, around my brother's old bedroom. "Where do you think we can buy a torch round here?" I had a plan.

"Let's have a look, there must be garage or somewhere that sells them; it's a dark enough place."

Chapter Seventeen
The Windmills of Your Mind

We approached The Inn, late in the afternoon. It appeared different to me that day, as though it had never belonged to me. Walking through the garden, all my time there faded into a tiny droplet of history; I felt insignificant.

Larry was sitting on one of the benches, by the door, with another man. "Hello girls, am I glad to see you," he said, looking genuinely pleased at our arrival, which lifted my spirits. "This is my partner, Martin," I caught Susan trying not to raise her eyebrows at this, as it was somehow clear that he didn't mean the business sort.

"Hi Martin, I'm Alice, and this is Susan," I said, leaning in to shake his hand. He was quite a few years younger than the three of us, and very fit.

"How are you doing, Larry?" Susan asked. "We've been worried about you."

"The brewery have been down to visit, and to cut a long story short, it doesn't look good for me. There's no sign of a forced entry, so what are they supposed to make of it all? It looks like I didn't lock up properly, when I know that I did."

"That's terrible," we both said. I felt awful that we were the last ones to leave The Inn, and hoped we hadn't put Larry off, in some way, causing him to forget to lock one of the doors. I didn't know if I should mention the intruder at the big house but decided to keep quiet for the time being.

"Is there anything we can do to help? We can always look after the bar for you," I asked, feeling a bit insincere offering our services, as I did have an ulterior motive.

"Oh no, you won't need to be doing that," he said firmly, but in a kind voice. "I've got two staff in tonight, and it's going to be a quiet one anyway. Let's just relax and enjoy ourselves." It appeared that he had already explained to Martin who I was but we filled in a few more details, about the last week, and kept him entertained with this.

"So, did you find anything interesting up there?" Martin asked, referring to our brief visit to the living accommodation.

I explained about the painting, and the one in the big house. I also asked if they had ever noticed the face in the glass of the small bedroom window.

"Well, I've never seen that before. Have you Larry?" Martin's curiosity at this was clear from his expression.

"I can't say that I have, perhaps we should go and take a look," as he said this, I couldn't believe my luck; no awkward request would be necessary to take another peek upstairs.

We made our way through the empty bar, and up the stairs, where we were soon gathered around the painting of Cornelius Walker. I explained how the name now made sense; that my brother and I had called the ghost of The Inn 'The Night Walker'. We then went into my old room and showed them the photo on Susan's phone, of the man in the hat. Martin leant out to take another one, and we all inspected the unusually wide, interior window ledge.

We wondered if the image in the glass wasn't another one of Cornelius, and then questioned his relationship to Mrs Napper and her nephew; the troublesome Samuel Walker. They had to be descendants of his, by some line or other.

"Would you mind if we take a look at my brother's old room?" I asked, as this didn't seem such an out of place request at this point.

"Not at all, although, I think you'll find things a little different in there now; won't they, Martin?" As they smiled, knowingly at each other, I had no idea what to expect.

Susan tentatively opened the low door, on the other side of the landing. We were surprised to see that the long room was now an artist's studio, and very neatly arranged. Layers of large, oil painted canvases of local scenes were propped up against the walls; we marvelled at his skill. There were many of the beach, and the surrounding areas, caught in different weather conditions; Turneresque in method.

"These are breathtaking, you are very talented," I said, not expecting this at all, and feeling quite amazed at the changes made to my brother's old room.

Susan was equally awestruck. "These are fantastic, Martin. You really capture the energy of everything in your sight. I can hardly believe my own eyes."

"There, don't I always tell you the same?" Larry beamed, patting Martin on the back; who, looking quite embarrassed at all the fuss, began to fiddle about with some of his brushes, arranging them in their pots.

"Feel free to have a look around; I'll have to get used to it, as I've got some of them at an exhibition in Cromer soon."

"I think you should cast your net wider than that; London is where I would take these," Susan added, enthusiastically.

Just then, I came upon a pile of ink and watercolour sketches of people, in a grotesque style; quite unlike his other work. As I looked through them I found one of Sam Walker, or at least, I thought it was him. He appeared to be lurking around some old farm buildings, near the last entrance to the great house, on Beach Road, as it heads down towards the sea.

"Martin, could you have a look at this with me?" I asked, wanting to be sure of what I was looking at.

"Oh no, those are just experiments; I've been dabbling with figures. I'm afraid I'm not very accomplished at those."

"Well perhaps these might mean something to you Larry? Come over here and take a look at this."

"Well, if it isn't?" he also appeared to recognise him. "What's he up to?"

"What have I done?" Martin asked, confused.

"That's Sam Walker," Larry said, on taking a look, also perplexed at the drawing.

"I don't know who these people are; I just take the photos and have a go at them later."

This was all very interesting but I realised I was getting drawn away from my original purpose. I wanted to have a look behind the fake wall, at the little tunnel.

"I don't know quite how to put this," I began, "but when we lived here this was my brother's bedroom. We used to crawl around the passage that was inadvertently made at some time, by lessening the drop from the ceiling with a false wall; we used to put things in there."

"What sort of things?" Martin asked, looking amused at this.

"That's just it; I'm not really sure what we left in there, and I would like to know."

"Well, I've never seen any entrance to anything in here," Larry said, looking perplexed.

"Just behind here, there are two lumps," Martin moved some of his canvases and started tearing away the wallpaper.

"Steady on there, Martin!" Larry looked as shocked at his flurry of activity as I felt.

"I want to know what's in there. Don't you?"

He revealed two small metal fittings and turned them with some effort, before stepping back, as the flimsy sheet of hardboard fell at his feet. "Voila, there's your passage."

I took my newly purchased torch from my rucksack and crawled in there. I had imagined this moment for decades. Without the Doctor to keep a look out, my new friends stood guard. It was, in fact, the first time I had entered this long yet small space without the fear of being caught.

The light revealed the red brick of the wall on one side, the hardboard and supporting wooden frames opposite, and the old floorboards; which were darker than their extremities which extended into the room. With only the knowledge that my knees were in for a hard time, I began the lengthy crawl. I found it hard to believe that we used to make solo explorations of this with the tiny torch; it must have been very frightening. The entrance was near the door to the room; in order to reach the end, I had to go right round the outside.

"Are you alright in there?" Larry called.

"Yes, I'm fine. I'll give on knock every now and then, so you know where I am," I said, tapping on the hardboard, as I reached the first corner.

At this point I became quite nervous, as the short side of the tunnel was draped with thick cobwebs, each of these obstructing my progress; using the back of the torch to clear them meant I was momentarily unable to see ahead. I hoped their architects were long gone.

Tapping to announce my arrival at the second corner and, feeling the pressure of the darkness behind me, I pushed on to the end.

Approaching my destination, I caught sight of a child's shoe box and paused. I so wanted to remember what treasures we had placed in there were before opening it; I had recalled so many details and couldn't understand why something so significant was mostly lost to my mind.

I shone the light on the box; it had belonged to a pair of boy's 'Wayfinders'. I remembered going on the train to Norwich, with my mother and brother, in order to purchase these, special shoes, for him. They had soles which left big cat paw prints, and a compass was concealed in one heel.

The inky faces of a scout, a cub and a smartly-tied schoolboy gazed at me from the crumbling, green and cream cardboard, as I held my hands over it, in an anticipation mixed with dread. The great moment had arrived. With the torch in one hand, I carefully lifted the lid and shone its light on the contents of the box. Inside there were many coca cola bottle caps; I then had the vague recollection that we marked each visit with one of these splendid offerings, snaffled from the bar. Rifling amongst them, I found the long, blue box of my Timex watch; a few childish drawings, on scraps of paper; and, much to my surprise, one key attached to a black leather key ring, bearing a silver, winged and circled letter M, set in a red, enamelled background. I placed this item in my pocket.

Knocking triumphantly on the hardboard, I crawled my way back, with the shoe box tucked gently under my left arm. As I reached the end of the tunnel, I noticed something we never could have seen with our tiny torch; there was something after our exit that suggested a passage to somewhere else.

I returned to my brother's old room and placed the shoe box carefully on the work bench, next to Martin's brushes. "There's something you should all see," they gathered round, looking expectantly at the box, "No, it's not in there. Come with me."

They followed me back into the passage. "What do you make of this?" I scanned the old panelling, at the back wall, just past the entrance we had come through, with the light of the torch. There were two little dips, like thumb prints, in the old wood; in a section at the drop of the roof. It was very low down, but if removed, there would be just enough space for a person to fit through, with some effort. Martin, instinctively, pushed his thumbs into the marks; the panel fell inward, slightly.

We all crouched back; seeking each other's response to this, in the partial darkness.

"Is it a secret doorway?" Susan whispered, stooping her way forward to inspect it. She and Martin felt around the rest of the panel to see if anything would make it move, but to no effect.

"There must be something behind here, in the gap," placing her hand into the unseen space and groping about.

Martin put his hand in the other side. "I think I've got something here," as he said this, the top of the panel dropped forward again, and the lower edge was propelled in and up; they just about managed to get their fingers clear of its violent action. "God, that was close. Are you alright, Susan?"

Susan clutched her arm to her chest, "I'll be fine; I slammed the back of my hand, pulling it out."

"The torch please, Alice," Martin said, with a confidence that reminded me of the Doctor, "I'm going in."

"Well, alright, but I'm coming behind you." I wasn't going to miss out on this.

I followed him, again on my knees, into what was an even smaller passage than the one around the room. Unable to see what was before me, apart from the occasional glimpse of brickwork caught in the torch light, around his silhouette, I blindly pursued Martin,

"We must be below the window in the spare room, your old room, by now," my face met with his muscular backside, as he stopped suddenly. "It looks like there is another exit here, in front of me; that would take us into Larry's room."

"That's my parents' old room", I called out, thinking about 'The Night Walker' and his nocturnal ramblings. This must have been how he either got in there or gave them, and the dog, the impression that someone was in there with them.

"There's been so much work done on that room, I don't think we'll be able to get through," he shone the torch back at me and then down, onto the floorboards around us.

"Can you back up a bit, Alice?"

I reversed as quickly as I could.

"I think I've found something," with this there was some fumbling about, for what seemed like a long time, before the quiet thud of wood on wood reached my ears.

"There's a way down."

I squeezed forward, closely pressed against Martin, as he scanned the light around the hole he had revealed. Looking down, on one side of this there were rough planks, making a vertical ladder, fixed to the wall.

"I'll find my footing and shine the torch up at you."

"Ok," I said feeling anything but this, as I tried to get my bearings, believing that we were next to the fireplace, in the saloon.

Eventually, when I reached the bottom rung and Martin span the torch around, looking for a way out. There was a reel of thin rope, attached to a mechanism; it must have been the same type as the one that let us in here. It took him a moment to work it out, and then we were through.

Chapter Eighteen

No Time

We weren't in the saloon, but instead found ourselves in the beer cellar, that was actually on the ground floor; behind The Inn and the living accommodation.

"I don't see how this could have been used in the burglary, as nothing was taken from the cellar, and we didn't manage to get into the bar," I said, thinking out loud.

"I was considering that myself," Martin answered, moving the torch about the walls and ceiling. "It wouldn't surprise me if that wasn't the only secret passage though."

"I believe you could be right," I said, feeling quite certain of this.

Martin turned on the light. As I scanned the walls my eyes fell upon an old clock, the hands of which were fixed together, for eternity, at twelve o'clock.

"Oh no, I'd completely forgotten! I'm supposed to meet Rachel and Don at nine o'clock. Do you know what time it is?"

"It's nine-fifteen."

"Sorry Martin, I've got to go," I spluttered, trying to open the door but it was locked from the outside.

"The only way out now is by the way we came in," he said looking amused and, at the same time, concerned by my state of panic.

All the way back, I worried that they would be angrier with me than they had been that morning. I clambered fearlessly, and at quite a pace, up the rungs in the wall, without a care for the drop below or the darkness, but when we made our way through the tiny tunnel, Martin kept stopping to explore panels and floorboards; I had to keep him moving.

"Please Martin, hurry up," I said, giving him an energetic shove on the backside.

"You do know I'm spoken for?"

"Very funny, young man, now please move your arse," I felt my heart thudding in my ears, as we emerged into the bedroom.

"Well that's odd, they've gone."

"I can see that," I said, making a grab for the shoebox, before rushing out and downstairs to The Inn.

I lifted the hinged section of the bar, and was about to make a run for the door, when I felt all eyes were on me. Even my own reflection stared back from the other side of the room; cobwebs decorated my hair; my eyes looked slightly mad; and, to add to this, I was desperately clutching the tatty old box. Taking a deep breath, and trying to regain my composure, I spotted Susan, Larry, Rachel and Don, huddled round a small table by the door; they were also looking at me.

"A pint is it, Alice?" Don asked, and they all laughed at this, and at me I imagined.

"I'll get that," Martin called from behind the pumps.

I noticed Susan had an ice pack on her hand; Rachel followed my eyes to this and then gave me the once over. "I can see you two have been busy," she said, sarcastically.

"You could say that," I answered, pulling up a stool and perching uncomfortably on it.

"What's all this about shoe boxes and tunnels?" Don said, grinning broadly at me; this was a relief.

"Things just seem to happen to me," I shrugged.

"Do they now?" Rachel added.

I was glad to see Martin arrive at this point, with two pints of foaming ale; probably a little too much head, but I wasn't going to quibble about that.

"Well, that was interesting," he said, before pulling up a seat at the next table, and taking a long drink after handing me mine. "Have you ever heard anything about secret passages here before?" he asked, looking at Rachel and Don. I assumed he was an outsider as well.

"It's the kind of thing we heard about as kids, but not something any one has actually found, to my knowledge. Isn't that right Rachel?" Don appeared genuine enough.

"If anything, if I'm right in this, any talk of them was more associated with the big house," Rachel thought about this as she spoke; I could see her mind ticking over.

Martin began to fill them in with details of our exploration, as I stared around the saloon, feeling out of place and looking for my lost self. After a while I remembered the shoe box and decided to examine the little pieces of paper. The first one I unfolded was a very faint drawing; it appeared to be of a man. I wondered if it was 'The Night Walker', but he looked too nice, if it was possible to discern this from the childish lines. I stared at it, trying to recapture the intention of myself, or my brother, in creating this odd image.

The man was wearing a bow tie, and a frilled fronted shirt; my father often wore such clothes, but I believed that this was after we had left The Inn. Besides this, he had quite a full head of wavy hair, which my father did not possess, at any time.

The second was a crudely drawn map. It was clearly of The Inn, the big house, gatehouse and caravan site. One of the caravans was marked with a cross.

When I opened the final effort, I was shocked to see a single sentence, written in crayon. It read 'We know what you're up to!' I was impressed by the spelling and punctuation; I knew this had to be by my brother's hand.

"What have you got there?" Rachel asked.

"Oh, they're nothing; just some childish drawings," I was lying again.

"Did you remember to bring the keys?" she asked, bluntly. It appeared, if I wasn't going to give anything away, neither was she.

"What keys?" Martin asked, "To what?"

"They're to the big house, of course," she replied to him but smiled at Susan and me.

Feeling more than a little deflated at our missed opportunity, I pulled the keys from my pocket and handed them to her.

"What's this?" she said looking confused, raising the solitary key on the black leather fob for everyone to see. I had put it in the same pocket and produced it, accidentally, with the rest of them. "Is it one of yours, Don?"

"Now, let me see," he took it in his hand, studying it carefully. "No, this belongs to a Matchless; I don't have one of those. I didn't have you down as a biker, Alice"

"It's not mine, exactly," I said, knowing I had been caught out.

"Well, where did it come from?" Rachel asked.

"Here," I lifted the box, apologetically.

"And do you know who it really belongs to?" Don said, lowering his tone.

"I think I've got an awful idea as to who it might," I had a sinking feeling.

"And you're probably right," he looked gravely at me.

"This is all very interesting, but can we get to the point," Larry had apparently had enough of mysteries for one day.

"Only one person had a Matchless round here, back then," I knew what he was going to say, "And that was Sam Walker; it was his twenty-fifth birthday present from Mrs Napper. No wonder he was pissed off with you two little-un's!"

"Oh! Alice, you didn't? What ever were you thinking?" Rachel was barking up the wrong tree here; I had no idea how the key came to be in the box. Well, not at that moment, at least.

"We don't want that, you'd better take it back," Don passed the key to Rachel, and she slammed it on the table.

"It's getting late now; can we talk about this tomorrow?" I really was feeling very tired and wanted to sleep this day off. There was so much to take in and I was going to have to think very carefully about it all.

We made our way back to the gatehouse, with Susan supporting her injured hand, while I held the incriminating box at arms length. I was beginning to believe Judith Cunningham's mother might have been right about me. I always thought we only took innocent tokens, like the bottle tops; a motor bike key felt like theft. I couldn't believe we had done this. I didn't bother bolting the bedroom door and lay sleepless for a long time, trying to put the things I knew into some sort of order.

Despite the attempt to confuse him with the 'paranormal investigators', it seemed clear that Sam Walker knew he was under suspicion for the thefts from The Inn. I believed that we left the things at the end of the tunnel as offerings to 'The Night Walker', and the items I now had seemed to back this up; the cross on the map probably marked out his caravan, and the 'we know what you're up to' note must surely have been directed at him. I wondered if we knew his surname was Walker, even so, from my memory we also feared the Walker in the paintings; unless we saw them as one person.

This idea began to interest me. Could we have thought that Sam Walker was a time traveller? We were quite obsessed by the possibility of them; I say possibility, but we believed in them. Or did 'we'? My brother did like a bit of fun at my expense, as is common with the older sibling, in my experience at least. I really was going to have to ask him about this and risk a ribbing.

My thoughts wandered around the other things I had found out, looking for clues. Judith Cunningham and Sam Walker's cub sprang to mind. If he was so bad, how was she so nice, or was she? All I knew was that he brought her up in his commune and that she could sing. What was his commune like and where was it?

I must have fallen asleep at some point, as I was eventually ambushed on my own pillow.

"Good morning girls, I thought you might like a cup of tea," I woke to this, and the rattle of crockery on a tin tray. I thought I was back at the bungalow. It was Rachel.

"I let myself in; you've got a busy day ahead. No time for snoozing."

"What have you got in mind?" I felt alarmed and wondered where this would lead us. I had my own plans but these would have to wait.

"A few things, Alice, but first I'm afraid I have some sad news," she looked like she had been crying. "I've been up all night. I got a call from the nursing home and I'm sorry to say that Mrs Napper passed away this morning."

"Oh no, how sad," Susan said, sitting up.

"You need to get dressed now and meet me at the butler's apartment," Rachel ordered, and with this, she left.

"I don't like this at all," I said, turning to Susan, "I've been hoping something would happen, but not this."

"I know what you mean. Come on, we'd better get ready and see what she wants."

Chapter Nineteen
Pagan Baby

We found Rachel sitting in the middle of the pentagram, on the kitchen floor, in her formerly, happy home. Her eyes were fixed on the bunch of keys, spread out, deliberately, at her feet.

"Rachel, are you alright?" I was worried about her, as I could see that she had slipped into the past, just as I had done during the last week or so. She didn't acknowledge us.

"Rachel," Susan said, crouching down and putting an arm around her shoulders, "we're here."

"So you are," she said abruptly. "Let's go upstairs now."

I knew something was very wrong with her, as we followed. She wafted up the stairs and along corridors, just as she had done during the ghost walk of the village, but this time without the commentary.

When we arrived at the doors to the room of the plant watering, it was in darkness, despite it being a sunny morning. I quickly realised that the wooden shutters to the windows were closed and noticed a familiar silhouette at the far end of the room.

"Are we ready?" the figure spoke.

"We are," Rachel replied.

"Will someone, please, tell me what is going on?" I asked, beginning to feel uncomfortable.

"Alice, you know Gail?", as I adjusted my eyes, she came towards me pushing the old bath chair that I had wheeled Mrs Napper around in all those years ago.

"Sit down, please," Gail said, gesturing towards the chair.

"It's alright Alice, I'm here," Susan stepped in. "What on earth is going on?"

"You aren't the only one with a little box of secrets," Rachel said, looking my way. "Mrs Napper also had one, and told me on her death bed, to ask Alice where it is. She couldn't remember where she had put it, but when I told her a few days ago, that you had returned to the village, she remembered showing you."

"I know nothing." I replied, amazed at this suggestion.

"Precisely, I thought this would be the case; that's why Gail is here. I can hypnotize but she's much better than me."

"Hold on now," Susan added, "isn't this going a bit far?"

"No, we need her to remember," Rachel snapped.

Having never been hypnotized before, I began to find the idea quite appetizing, although I was concerned about what the result of this might be. I also thought of my parents warning me about the locals, and knew they would find my current situation quite ridiculous.

"Let's give it a go," I said, laughing, and with a creak of wicker, found myself sitting in the bath chair. I put my hands on the tiller, vaguely recalling this position, and realised that I must have been allowed to sit in it before.

"Let go of that now," Gail ordered, "I want you to empty your mind and relax."

There was some counting back, and a bit of clenching this and that body part, before I was aware of Gail's voice asking me to have a yawn and open my eyes.

"Was that it?" I asked, as Rachel folded back the shutters and light flooded the room.

"Yes, we've finished," Gail said, looking at Rachel and then Susan. They both appeared dumb struck.

"Did we find the hiding place of the box?" I had a feeling we hadn't.

"No, we did not," Rachel answered.

"Oh well, at least we tried," I said, feeling rather relaxed. "That's the best nap I've had in ages, thanks Gail."

"Is there nothing you remember about this room; anywhere special Mrs Napper might have shown you?" Rachel asked, looking quite defeated.

"No, not a thing comes to mind, although, this does remind me of the other night."

"What do you mean, the other night?" Gail gasped, clutching her wrist, as though it twitched with pain at the mention of this.

"We saw a light scanning this room, as though someone was searching for something."

"I didn't tell you Gail," Rachel added, "they saw what they thought was an intruder in the house, the night before The Inn was burgled."

"Did you?" she looked accusingly at Susan and myself.

"This is getting us nowhere," Rachel said, impatiently. "Oh, for God's sake, Alice, can't you remember anything?"

"No, I'm afraid I can't," with that we were hastily ushered back downstairs and out. Rachel slammed the gate, causing the little bell to jingle aggressively, after telling us that we would see her later.

"What the hell did you make of that?" I asked Susan, as we peered through the turnstile, watching Rachel stomp towards the house.

"I have no idea," she replied, looking as nonplussed as I felt.

I spent the rest of the morning typing a lengthy email to my brother, the Doctor, telling him all that had happened and hoping for even the tiniest nugget of information that he might decide to share, amidst the sarcastic response I anticipated.

"Do you think we could get some lunch now?" Susan asked, her head popping up from behind the book she was been reading, the one I had bought for my parents. "I'm starving, let's go to The Inn."

Larry and Martin were nowhere to be found; I was quite disappointed at this, knowing how entertained they would have been by my hypnosis. As we chewed our way through another ploughman's, Susan suddenly asked, "Who is Arthur?"

"Arthur?" I couldn't think of anyone by this name.

"When you were in a trance you kept asking about him, and saying that you couldn't see him."

"Well, that's a bit creepy. I can't think who he could be," I shuddered, almost choking on my pickled onion.

"What else did I say?" I had completely forgotten that my little blabber mouth had been in action, without my being able to at least listen to what it was spouting.

"Does 'my lovely home' ring any bells?" from the expression on her face, I believed I had used this phrase several times.

"Oh dear," I wasn't expecting that, "to cut a long story short, my landlord wants me out of the small house that I rent. He's got planning permission for flats."

"That's terrible, Alice."

"It is, and I don't see how I'll be able to afford to stay in London now."

I had been trying to put this out of my mind, knowing that the time to go back and deal with the situation was getting closer, but this was not the time to dwell on my own problems. Something was clearly going on here, more than our search to uncover the secrets of my past.

"Susan, why do you think Rachel and Gail are in such a state?"

"I have been wondering the same thing. Even if Rachel had to spend the night seeing Mrs Napper out, this seems more than sadness at that. Rachel is a tough old bird; I don't get it."

"That's exactly what I've been thinking; that box must be of some importance to them both. Anyway, we're not going to find anything out sitting here."

"Let's find Larry and Martin, there must be another hole somewhere for you to go down," Susan said, looking excited at this prospect.

We asked at The Inn but were only told that they were both out, so instead we decided to walk down Beach Road, to try and find where Martin had taken the photo of Sam Walker. Just after the flint wall of The Inn and the former grounds to the big house ended there were three new town houses, and then a deserted farm house with out-buildings; and yet another planning application for redevelopment, this time for the farm.

"This is becoming a familiar theme," Susan said sadly, looking at me.

"It certainly is," the gate was padlocked, so I climbed over. "Come on Susan, he must have been in here for a reason."

"Perhaps it was a call of nature?"

"If I'm right, he was crouching down about here," I found a spot that seemed similar to the one in the photo, by the eaves of the barn at the front.

"There's nothing remarkable here, perhaps he was waiting for someone?"

We walked around for some time, taking in the eerie, yet beautiful, place; some of the buildings were so old they should surely have been listed. The main barn sagged into the ground; the land beneath it having shifted under the weight of two centuries or more. The skeletons of unrecognisable farming equipment had rotted into the earth around them; no doubt left tenderly in their final resting places, by the owners, on what I imagined must have been a sad day.

Susan had her hands cupped to the glass of a window, at the front of the farm house. "Come over here," she whispered, "it looks as though someone has been staying here recently."

A gas camping stove stood on the old range, two earthenware cups and wooden bowls were laid out neatly on the table in the middle of the room; while a clothes horse, draped with t-shirts, socks and pants, sat beneath the window.

"Never mind recently, I think they must still be here," I gripped Susan's arm, ready to pull her away.

"What the hell are you doing?" an angry male voice shouted out behind us. I turned around in horror, only to see Larry and Martin, laughing their heads off.

"Thanks for that, like we need shaking up any more than we already have been," I joked, but could just as easily have burst into tears. I realised that the long nights were catching up with me.

"Well, what have we got here?" Larry asked.

"Trespassers or squatters, unless I'm mistaken; make of it what you will," I said, regaining my composure.

"And I wonder who they might be?" Larry clearly knew exactly who was staying there.

"Could that be Sam Walker, perhaps, and a friend?" Susan suggested.

"Sam Walker and a daughter; more like," he said, sounding quite certain of this, "They're in the village, and I can't see that they're stopping anywhere else."

"Doesn't he have a commune somewhere?" I wondered how much Larry knew about the mysterious Mr Foxy.

"He did have, it was in some fields, just outside Cromer, full of old buses and tents for years; until the land owner saw a profit in it and turned it into one of those retreats, with yurts and yoga classes."

I was suddenly filled with empathy for Mr Foxy; whatever he had done.

"I've never really had a look around the gatehouse," Martin proclaimed, out of the blue.

"As you've shown us yours, I think we can return the favour," Susan said, smiling to herself.

We walked back up Beach Road, stopping to look at the grinning man in the casement window, who appeared to be mocking us. Larry then groaned about the lack of trade, as we passed through The Inn garden, and before long we were standing outside the side entrance to the gatehouse.

"When you look at it all from here, you realise what a huge area this all covers," Martin said, thoughtfully.

"I've been thinking the same thing," I marvelled at the space, as I had done on my arrival. Looking up at the big house I pictured Mrs Napper and my little self, gazing back at us.

"Did you hear that Mrs Napper died last night?"

"No, we hadn't," Larry appeared strangely amused by this news. "Now, that's going to open up a can of worms."

"What do you mean?" Susan asked.

"The house is held in trust by a corporation, something to do with Mr Napper's side of the family, but there's often been talk of deeds, and other versions of wills, kept somewhere by Mrs Napper. I wonder if they'll be lost forever or reappear now she's gone."

"Why would she have kept them hidden?" I wondered aloud.

"Who knows, perhaps they would have affected her rights to the place?"

I left Susan and Larry to show Martin around, while I checked to see if there had been a response from my brother, to the email. There was. All he had sent back was a picture of a Great Dane and I thought it might be one of his jokes. I then took out the little pieces of paper from the shoe box and was studying them when Martin returned.

"It's all very nicely decorated but I don't think I'd fancy staying in that bedroom; it's even creepier than those at The Inn. What have you got there?"

"Just a picture, either my brother or I drew it, when I was about six."

"Let me see," I reluctantly handed it over to the great artist.

"I thought it might be of 'The Night Walker', although he looks too friendly, or Mr Napper, but I'm sure I didn't know what he looked like."

"No," he replied thoughtfully, "I don't believe it's either of them."

Larry reappeared with Susan, "Come on, let's go back to The Inn; Martin can knock us up a bit of dinner."

Over our meal we considered recent events. "We've got the setting but let's see where all the characters fit into it. Let's go through all the people you've been involved with since you came back here," Susan suggested, lifting her glass.

"You are quite the detective now, Martin," Larry chuckled, over his pint pot. "What's your take on all of this?"

Martin smirked and gestured to me, "Let's hear what Miss Marple's got to say."

"Thank you, Martin," I coughed, giving him a rude salute. "Rachel and Don would be the first. I'm wondering why Rachel is so bothered by Mrs Napper's demise; perhaps that has something to do with the deeds. She does own two places on the property," I believed this could be relevant.

"We could be getting somewhere. Was Gail next, what about her?" Susan wasn't partial to 'The Circle'.

"No, but she's tied in with Sam Walker, whatever he means to her now. No, it was Judith Cunningham I saw after Rachel and Don. She was looking at the big house, on the open day for its redevelopment into retirement apartments."

"Do you think she might be looking for somewhere to be with her mother, now she's getting on a bit?" Susan added.

"Now, you'd think that, wouldn't you," of course, he would know, as that bar seems to have been a hotbed of information for years; I could see how my parents would have been irritated by this.

"Come on Larry, spill the beans," Martin was so obviously amused by the whole thing.

"Mother Cunningham owns a house down Cart Lane, she used to take in holiday boarders; it's big enough for Judith and her old man to live in with her without ever having to rub shoulders too much. If she was coming back to look after her, they'd be living there. No, either she was being nosy or she has other interests in the place."

"What about Sam Walker and his daughter, Agnes?" I was increasingly fascinated by the pair. "Where might they fit into the recent activity?"

"Not forgetting that Sam was Edith's nephew. They come by, every now and then, so that Agnes can make a bit of money with her little band; playing up and down the coast, staying here and there," he paused for a moment. "I have no idea how Sam makes money, but when I think about it, he's always here when those witches are around."

"While we're here, do you think we could have another look at your paintings, Martin?" Susan asked. "It might also be interesting to see all the photos you've taken. Larry and Alice may see things in them that you wouldn't have noticed."

"That sounds like an excellent idea," Larry agreed, getting into this sleuthing business.

We went upstairs and back to my brother's old room, where Susan entertained herself by selecting different landscapes and setting them on the easel to study them, while Larry and I worked our way through the vast collection of photos; all arranged in folders of different categories. Martin settled down in one corner with a sketch pad, and I had the uncomfortable feeling we were being observed with an artist's eye but left him to it.

One of the folders had been given the title 'orbs', with a large question mark after the word. This contained many photos of The Inn and surrounding areas, with balls of light, sometimes one, and occasionally, several, appearing in them.

"Bloody hell, Martin," Larry called across to him, holding up the folder, "maybe the old place is haunted?"

"They're probably specks of dust, caught by the light, but who knows?" he returned to his drawing. "I like them, anyway."

Another folder, named 'characters', was mostly of individuals in routine situations, with the odd one including people in conversation. Unwittingly, Martin had caught Gail and Sam Walker involved in a heated discussion outside 'The Circle'.

"Now, this is interesting," taking his time to consider the image, Larry then looked surprised by it. "As far as I know, these two never speak to each other. I wonder what's going on here; when would you have taken this?"

"Just look on the back, they're all dated," Martin answered, without lifting his head.

"It's from this time last year," I noticed.

"Another visit from the witches probably coincided with it, I'll bet," this was a good piece of work. "I'd love to know what they were arguing about," Larry said, with a grin.

"Well, we can hardly ask them," Susan threw in.

"No, but Rachel seems quite cosy with Gail. Maybe she knows?" I imagined how awkward it would be, confronting her with the photo but decided that we should keep it, just in case a suitable opportunity arose. I put it in my pocket, nodding to Larry.

We went downstairs, as it was time for Larry to help behind the bar. I sat with Susan and Martin, having a drink at our table by the door.

"Let's play building detectives," Martin suggested. So, to the curiosity of the customers, we spent the next hour going in and out of the building, gauging the thickness of the walls against the interior dimensions. This proved a fruitless, yet enjoyable, activity.

Closing time arrived, and as we were about to make our way back to the gatehouse, Martin gave me a rolled piece of paper.

"The mystery man, from your drawing, I believe?"

So this was what Martin had been sketching; I opened it up to reveal a perfect drawing of Jon Pertwee; as Doctor Who.

"Compare it with your picture, and I think you'll see I'm right."

"How funny, that explains something else. Perhaps the drawing that shocked everyone was also of him. It's a long story; I'll explain it to you another time. Look Susan, the sonic screw driver looks like a knife in his chest. That's hilarious, thanks Martin."

Another mystery had been resolved.

Chapter Twenty

Helter-skelter

Before long, Susan was snoring, and grinding her teeth; she probably had a lot of information to chew over. I, on the other hand, found sleep a difficult friend to locate, and so, surveyed the room; knowing that someone had got in here by some means. When our things had been moved around downstairs, I believed that someone may have come in with a key, but after finding the tunnel at The Inn, I was convinced that I hadn't been sleep walking, opening drawers or upsetting the chair; there had to be a way into this room when the door was bolted.

I got out of bed and felt around the walls in the darkness, but they revealed nothing. I thought about the structure of the building and considered how the stairs approached the door, and that the panelling of these was completely sealed. This was a waste of valuable space in such a small house; usually a cupboard would be made under the rise of the stairs, but there wasn't one. Using my torch, I surveyed the floor boards by the door. There were two definite notches, at the outside edges of three planks. I put my fingers in and tried to lift them, to no avail; this would have been too easy and obvious.

Trying to imagine someone needing to escape this room in a hurry, I stood with my back to the bolted door. I shone the torch light in front of my feet and saw a small scoop made into the wood, I instinctively thrust my heel into it and the boards rose at the other end, with a click.

Two iron supports held the floor ajar. I unlatched these and lifted the boards back, unveiling a dark space. Pointing the light of my torch downwards, I saw planks, like the ones at The Inn, again providing a ladder of sorts.

Hurriedly, I put on my boots before starting my decent, and with no one to watch my back, I felt nervous, yet liberated.

Counting thirty rungs, I knew that I must have been way below the ground floor. Eventually, my foot met with a stone surface; I had reached the bottom. Turning around, I shone the torch on a tall tunnel, about three feet in width. Able to stand with ease, I was amazed to see that this was built in the same brick as the gatehouse.

I considered going back and waking Susan, but didn't. Instead, I chose to live in the moment that had found me, and made my way along as silently as I could; although, the sound of my own breathing was amplified by the arched ceiling.

Before long, I found myself in a larger area, and, moving the torch around, I could see that it was a circular space, with the dark mouths of identical entrances, facing each other in the now more rugged walls. Then, skimming the floor with the light, I became alarmed at the appearance of an increasingly familiar image, that of a pentagram drawn with chalk. It was surrounded by wilting, cut foliage and spent tea lights in small glasses. Feeling disorientated, I became confused as to which entrance I had emerged from. With my heart thumping furiously, I was trying to decide which one to take, when a dim light appeared; getting closer and brighter, heading towards me from the entrance facing me. I bolted into the nearest tunnel, turned off my torch and began feeling my way along; too frightened to look back.

Despite the tunnel seeming to continue, I discerned an alcove in the wall; groping around in this there seemed to be more rungs going up. Knowing this wasn't the way back to the gatehouse, I had little choice but to climb and see where this led me.

My heart plummeted when I arrived at the top, as instead of a side exit there were two metal fittings, similar to the ones under the floor of the bedroom in the gatehouse, but now above me. They wouldn't budge, as I tried desperately to move them, one by one, whilst still holding the torch. Realising that I would have to lift them simultaneously, I placed the torch between my knees. Just as they clicked up and open, the torch dropped to the ground. I shot through the small space, lifting the boards with my head, and then slammed them shut behind me.

I instantly recognised where I was. Moonlight cast itself through tall windows, spreading out in patches along an oak floor, and just behind me was a large, stone fireplace, and I knew that I was in the big house; 'The End House'.

Rushing to the nearest window, in an attempt to work out which side of the building I was on, I saw The Inn, shrouded in darkness; with not one light on in the old place. I imagined Martin and Larry, sleeping peacefully, while Susan snored away at the gatehouse, probably dribbling on my pillow; all of them oblivious to my predicament.

Knowing that someone could pop up through the way I had come in, at any moment, I found my way down to the front door, but the brass knob resisted my hand; it had been locked with a key.

I headed back up the stairs, pausing briefly, to look at the image of Cornelius Walker. Those two work horses behind him, one dark and one grey, made me think of good and evil, and it now appeared to me as though he stood between them, making a scale; balancing the two forces.

I headed to the room I was most familiar with, the one of the plant watering; hoping that Susan, if she ever woke up, would see me at the windows.

That morning had been bizarre, the idea that I should remember anything through hypnosis, and that Mrs Napper had ever shown me her 'hiding place' almost made me laugh. Knowing I was stuck in there, I told myself that it was ridiculous to think that I was in any real danger. I would just have to see the night through, as best I could, and take advantage of the situation. I then remembered Gail's words, during the crystal ball reading; she had said that I would be alone in a dark place. I shuddered.

Standing with my back to the middle window in the huge room, contemplating the past and present, and almost returning to my Gail entranced state, I allowed Martin's collection of orb photographs to dance around my mind. Just as I noticed I was doing this, I seemed to have my eyes fixed on something similar, above the door. I span round, looking out of the windows, expecting to see a car head light, or something of that sort, but nothing was there.

I opened the door, recalling and retracing the steps I had once taken, behind that old bath chair. Moving through the entrance and into the corridor, I turned right, somehow remembering Mrs Napper explaining that this had been her husband's study. Very little furniture remained, even then; I could bring to mind only a desk and a round backed wooden chair, with a green leather seat and back pad, both of these rested on brass wheels; they had sat beneath the window which, I now saw, faced The Inn.

Back in the corridor of my dreams, I spied the room I remembered as Mrs Napper's. Although unlit and empty, I could picture a single bed with an elaborate wooden head board; the deep mattress covered with a pink, green and cream, flowery eiderdown. A silk rug stretched out and over the floor boards, whilst a tall, glossy wardrobe, with a long mirror, rose up between the two windows.

On the wall, there had hung an oil painting, set in a golden frame; the plaque at the bottom read, 'Edith and her brave Shannon'. It was Mrs Napper riding side saddle, on an elegant, iron grey horse. How the hell did I remember all this stuff? Gail was probably better than I'd given her credit for.

I became transfixed at the point on the wall where I believed the painting had once hung; even in the darkness there seemed to be a pale rectangle marking its absence. Crouching down, I let my fingers play along the skirting board, at the foot of the panelling beneath this spot; a small section of which came away in my hands, with little resistance. Fishing around in the space behind this, I came upon something cool and metallic. Taking it to the light of the window, I could see that it was a very old shortbread tin, with the reproduction of a painting on its lid; a kilted bagpipe player sat in one corner of a kitchen, leading a chorus of howling dogs.

For the second time, in as many days, I had found a collection of secrets; but this time not mine.

On prising the lid open, I discovered a layer of champagne and wine corks, at once knowing this must have been where I had got the idea of collecting the coca cola lids, and the idea for a secret hoard. Beneath these, there was a roll of creamy paper, with a broken wax seal; I unfurled it but found the curling inked script impossible to read in the dim light. There was a map, which also reminded me of the find in my own little box. Near the bottom I found two photographs, I lifted the first to the light and saw Mrs Napper, again on the grey horse, with a man, who I assumed to be Mr Napper, holding its head and smiling up at her. It was nice to see them happy. The second photograph was of a painting of a lady, in Georgian costume. Beneath these, was a layer of cloth, which I lifted and revealed a pendant on a heavy chain, with a label attached to it by a thread; I could just make out the word 'Walker' on this.

I placed the items back in the tin, closed the lid and slid down the wall falling onto the floor, exhausted. Cradling the treasure in the crook of my arm, I curled up on the cool wooden boards and drifted off to sleep.

"Wake up luv," I came too, seeing a pair of calf length, tan boots. My eyes moved further up, and I shot back in horror at the sight of the fox's head.

"Oh my God" I called out, terrified.

"Calm down there, I'm not going to hurt you," he said, quietly, sounding as if he meant this. "I found the torch, and thought I'd best see who it belongs to, that's all."

"You're Sam Walker?" I asked, knowing this to be the case; still in a state of panic.

"I am, and you're Alice," I was surprised by the soft sound of his voice, and that he knew who I was.

"Why were you down there?" I whispered, turning my fingers around the treasure, drawing it behind myself.

"I might ask the same question, but as you asked me, you could say I'm the keeper of the labyrinth," he said, stepping back. "Now, do you want to get out of here, or are you going to spend the night on that floor?"

"I think I want to get out of here," I stood up and, from the pressure of my grip, the tin fell to the floor, its contents scattering; Sam Walker appeared to ignore this, and my scrabbling around.

"I don't have a key, so it's back the way we came, I'm afraid. If you follow me, I'll get you safely to the gatehouse."

With the tin clamped safely beneath my arm, I again found myself going down a rabbit hole. Only this time, following my phantom, and all the way he kept checking on me.

"Mind how you go, not much further down now," his voice called out, reassuringly.

We passed along the first tunnel, through the circle and on, until eventually he pointed the light of his torch up the planks, which led back to the gatehouse.

Before I climbed up, he paused, putting a hand on my arm. "Now, in that tin, there may be things that I might be interested in, or belong to me, but I'm sure that when you've had a look at them you will know what to do."

"Thank you," I was unusually lost for words, still feeling very anxious, "but where will I find you?"

"You'll find me," he answered, and after pointing the torch up the ladder, to guide my first steps, Sam Walker disappeared into the darkness.

Chapter Twenty-one
I Woke Up

Susan was sitting at the foot of the bed. "Where the hell did this come from?" she asked, holding the paper with the broken seal, with the other contents of the tin spread over the duvet.

"It's a very long story," I sighed, falling back against the pillow, "but a cup of tea would be nice."

While Susan was downstairs, I read the document. The gist of it was that in eighteen-seventy, one Sebastian Walker had gambled away the house, all other buildings and grounds, to a Joseph Napper. This was interesting enough, but as I read on there was a clause, this being that it was for the length of one hundred years only, and that it should then be returned to the head of the Walker family. This was counter signed by Henry Gilmont, and some other names that were a bit smudged.

I was amazed. If this was still considered a legally binding document it could affect Rachel's ownership of the butler's apartment and the gatehouse in some way; there was no wonder that she was stressed about the possibility of its existence. And then, there was the development of the house, plus any claims Sam Walker might have on the place.

"Have you read this?" I asked, as Susan appeared with the tea tray.

"Yes, I have, but what are you going to do with it?"

After explaining the events of the previous night, I decided that we should tell no one about this until we had shown it to a solicitor. We then searched the internet and couldn't believe our eyes, when we soon came upon 'Gilmont, Gilmont and Associates, Solicitors', based in Cromer; they had to be the ones for us.

Taking the bus, I again relived my occasional journeys to school with Judith Cunningham, picturing us in our straw hats; wondering if she knew about this document and if she had her sights set on some sort of pay back, knowing of her relationship to Sam Walker. I was still concerned about how the outcome of my finding the document might affect Rachel and Don; if Mrs Napper wasn't the eldest and closest descendent of Sebastian Walker in nineteen seventy, and in the years after. I wondered if her father's purchases had been legally binding. Plus the fact that the butler's house had been bought even before the Napper's time was up.

We arrived in Cromer and strolled down a narrow street in the direction of the sea, searching for the office amongst the quaint buildings, admiring their original overhanging bow windows and plaster fronts; all painted, in some tradition, from a palette of pastel shades.

Our destination, however, was not one of these. Eventually we came upon a very serious, little Georgian building, in plain red brickwork. Above the clear glass, bull's eye windows there was a hand painted sign, similar to that of a pub, hanging out into the street; this bore the words 'Gilmont, Gilmont and Associates, Solicitors. Estd.1852'.

Taking a deep breath, I opened the narrow wooden door and stepped down into the reception room. A rather dapper young woman, sporting a light weight tweed jacket and Windsor knotted green silk tie, was the only person sitting at one of the three desks. Her blonde hair was cut short, in a nineteen thirties style, waved, with a neatly gelled fringe, in a curl above her right eye.

"Can I help you in some way?" she asked, with her heavy, plummy voice filling the air.

"It's just an enquiry, really," Susan spoke, noticing that I had temporarily lost the ability to do so.

"Please, take a seat," she gestured to the expensive looking, modern leather and steel chairs in front of her desk.

"We have an old document relating to 'The End House' in Wythrum, that we believe hasn't been seen for years, and wondered if it's still legally binding," I blurted, as I lowered myself into the surprisingly uncomfortable chair, producing the paper from my rucksack.

"That sounds fascinating, could I have a look at it?" she asked, appearing very animated at the possibility, leaning over her desk and taking it from my hand before I had responded. "How did you come by this?"

"Oh, it's a long story," Susan stepped in, before I could reply.

"This seems to have been written by my great-great-grandfather; would you mind if I borrow it, to show to my father?" she said, after a hasty read.

"I don't think we should leave it," I answered, suddenly feeling uneasy about this, and noticing Susan shuffling about awkwardly.

"If you insist, but it would be quite safe here," she smiled, but for some reason I could hear alarm bells ringing and wanted to get out of there, yet she had the document and was heading for the photo copier. When she returned, I made a grab for the original and left as quickly as we had arrived.

Emerging into the street Susan asked, "Are you thinking what I'm thinking?"

"Yes, if they were the solicitors for the Napper family back then, they might still be. What have I done?"

"We still have the original, but we need to find another solicitor, preferably one who has no interest in the Walker or Napper families."

Not trusting any of the plusher looking establishments, and after some trudging about, we found the sign for a practice, tucked away down an alley; it proclaimed that Hodges and Smythe specialised in conveyancing. I knew that this had something to do with property, so it seemed like a good choice.

I burst through the PVC door, rushed up the worn nylon-carpeted stairway and into the office, where I could see, whom I assumed to be, either Hodges or Smythe; having a crafty smoke outside the open fire exit.

"And you are?" he asked, exhaling.

"This is Susan, and I'm Alice. We've got an old document we'd like your opinion on." Between us, we explained the situation, and our visit to Gilmont, Gilmont and Associates.

"Well, this is interesting. I'm Adrian Hodges, by the way, and I would be very glad to pursue any claims made concerning of this contract," he said, peering self-assuredly over his half glasses.

"What will the fee be, for your services?" Susan sensibly enquired.

"Dependent on outcome, I would expect an appreciation of my efforts."

"It's settled then; can you take a copy and leave us with the original?" I was still suspicious that the disappearance of the document might be of no small value in some quarters.

"There's just one thing, do you have a member of the Walker family I can speak to?"

"Yes, there is someone" I couldn't believe I was talking about Samuel Walker.

We left our phone numbers, took a couple of his business cards and then took a stroll by the sea. I didn't want to return to the village before we had thought through what our next steps should be. I was of little doubt that the only person with any legitimate claims to the contents of the tin was Sam, but already felt that we had gone behind Rachel's back, in some way, by presenting the document to solicitors.

"The way I see it, Rachel told you that Mrs Napper wanted you to find the tin; didn't she actively try to bring this about with Gail?"

"Yes, that's true, but I think she hoped to be there at the time, and then it would have been hers; to do what she wanted with."

"Rachel isn't a member of the Walker family; the only ones we know of are Sam and his daughter, Agnes. It belongs to them, and you made a decision about what to do with it, just as he asked you to."

"This is also true. I think we should speak to Sam Walker, and have Larry and Martin present when we do."

"Yes, Larry is useful to Sam, as he lets Agnes and her group play at The Inn. That's a very good idea; I can see how he might be willing to do this but how do we find him again?"

"I don't know, he just said that I would be able to," but I couldn't imagine how.

After buying two impressive torches, we took the bus back to Wythrum, and went straight to The Inn.

When we arrived, we could see Larry and Martin in the car park; they appeared to be saying good bye to someone in an expensive looking black car. They didn't look very happy as they made their way towards us.

"That was the brewery rep, and it seems like I'm in deep trouble," Larry said, devoid of his usual upbeat manner.

"They're saying that Larry must have had an after hours party that got out of hand. What a load of rubbish," Martin said, looked affronted, for once.

"I think we've got a way to sort this out," Susan spoke, taking control of the situation, "Come to the gatehouse after closing time; we've got something to show you."

"I knew you'd have a plan, girls!" as he said this, the authentic Larry was instantly returned.

"Oh, and bring a couple of torches," I added.

"This sounds intriguing; I'm looking forward to it already," Martin replied, flashing a broad smile.

As we walked away, Susan asked, "And what about Rachel and Don?"

"We'll cross that bridge when we come to it," already dreading this, as I spoke.

In need of time to recover, we spent the rest of the day drinking tea and watching old films on the laptop. One in particular was too close to home; 'The Haunted House of Horrors' was the story of some friends visiting a Georgian mansion, where one of the characters had played as a child. It was curious to think that Gail had probably seen this; if what Rachel said about her fascination with ghostly dramas of the time was true.

By ten o'clock we were both quite bored. I didn't want to go to The Inn just in case Rachel and Don were there, which made me feel bad. We decided instead to take a walk around the place.

I was trying to remember how we had come by the motor bike key, belonging to Sam Walker. We went back to my little camp, behind the entertainment hall, where again, I crouched to my former height, looking at where the caravans had been. As I've already mentioned, we used to make cautious explorations of the areas we couldn't see from our view, and I tried to recall these.

I could picture the bike with the key left in it. Perhaps Sam Walker often did this, and such an occasion was the opportunity we had been waiting for. We might have wanted to immobilise him, for some reason, but there was another possibility; we might have just found it somewhere, known it was his and put it in our box to see if he would take it. This seemed more likely. We could have used it as bait for a trap.

"We should be getting back; it must nearly be closing time," with her words hanging in the air, Susan had already begun to walk away.

The End House, The Inn and gatehouse again took on a different atmosphere in the darkness. The daylight put them in the present, but they now appeared as they had been, long before my childhood. I looked at my feet, wondering which part of that underground structure lay beneath them, and could hardly believe that we would be down there very soon.

"Let's go and meet them, I could do with last orders," I said, feeling anxious; in the knowledge that I was reaching an ending.

As we entered the saloon, a few heads looked our way, and then turned inwards, making comments on our arrival; I imagined. Remembering the spectacle I'd made of myself, after my exploration with Martin, and on the night of the ghost walk, I realised that I couldn't really expect anything less.

"Alright there girls," Larry called out from behind the bar., "I'll bring you a drink over; we'll be finished here soon.

Instead, Martin arrived with a tray, "A double gin for Susan, and two pints of ale, for Alice and me. Is this Dutch courage?" he winked.

"Your guess is as good as mine, I don't know what to expect," Susan replied, shrugging her shoulders.

We made a ceremony of closing the place up, all following Larry and his bunch of keys; he was taking no chances.

"I have locked the side door," we all replied that he had. And so this went on, including the windows.

After walking to the gatehouse, with Martin and Larry bearing their torches, we went upstairs to the bedroom, collecting ours from the chest of drawers.

"What are we doing here?" Larry sounded confused.

"Just watch," Susan replied, tucking her arm into his, as I kicked, and then lifted the floor boards.

"Fantastic!" Martin whispered, turning on his torch again, and searching the hole with its beam, "Can I go first?"

"I was hoping you'd say that," I said, giving him a gentle shove.

Feeling safe due to their company, and yet nervous, I followed him down the aged rungs; with Susan, and then Larry behind us. All three of them were then awestruck at the sight of the impressive brickwork tunnel.

"Good heavens!" Larry exclaimed, "To think that someone built this; I wonder what it was for? I bet it was for smuggling."

"You're probably right there," Martin added, feeling the texture of the walls, "It's a serious tunnel."

No one spoke when we arrived at the circular space, until Susan called out, "Not another one," on spotting the pentagram.

Meanwhile, Martin was studying the walls. "Look at this part; it isn't brick, it's stone. This was a cave," he said, tracing his fingers around patterns, carved deep into its surface, "Either it was always below ground or the land above has been levelled off."

"And look at these," I moved my torch around, revealing the other tunnels.

"This is unbelievable," Larry said, shaking his head.

"So it is," a voice came from one of the tunnels, and we all turned to face Samuel Walker.

"Jesus!" Larry screamed, and then laughed, "You did give me a fright, you old dog."

Sam rocked around in hilarity and patted Larry on the back, "Cough it up, old boy!"

"What is this place?" Susan asked.

"And what do you do down here?" Martin added.

"It's the old Wythrum, to the witches, and I'm its keeper," Sam was beginning to sound like Rachel, doing one of her walks. "At the new moon of each season, the witches of Waltham come down here to return to their home, and I bring them."

"Why are they the witches of Waltham, if this is their home?" I had been wondering why they always came to Wythrum.

"That's where they fled to, when they were driven out by my ancestor, Cornelius Walker. I've been helping them come back for fifty years or so. They always came to the village, and working in the circle, I eventually put two and two together."

"When I lived at The Inn, did you use these tunnels to get in there?" I knew he had done.

"I went in there by chance; I only did it the once."

"Did you see me in my parents' bedroom?"

"I did, and wasn't I embarrassed; I hid in the passage waiting until you'd all gone to sleep."

"Did you move furniture around in the bar?" Susan asked.

"I might have done. The tunnel takes you in there and then you're a bit stuck, unless you know what you're doing," he looked amused and relieved to be telling us this, "Alice's dog kept barking on the other side of the wooden panelling, I thought he would give me away. There's a real warren around The Inn. Let me show you."

We all followed him down one of the tunnels, until we came to an alcove; similar to the one I went through the previous night.

Before we entered it, I asked, "Where does the rest of this tunnel lead to?"

"First things first, let's not confuse ourselves," he said, calmly leading us up the planks.

As Sam reached the top of the ladder, there was the sound of sliding stone and we emerged through the fireplace.

"No wonder we didn't find this one!" Martin exclaimed, "I don't suppose anyone used it very often."

"Desperate men in desperate times," Sam added, "Who would have thought of looking there? Well that was my way out, but it was mostly on the way further in that things would have to be moved around."

We stood in the middle of the saloon, looking round in the darkness, for where the next entrance could be.

"Any guesses?" Larry asked, sounding bewildered.

"So, we know that you had to move furniture around. Even though it was years ago, I'd imagine the tables fit naturally into certain places," Susan, as always, was on the ball.

I went to the corner table; the one Martin sat at the other night, next to our usual one; between the fireplace and the window.

"Well done, Alice," Sam said, moving the table and chairs, before sliding the lowest section of the panelling to one side.

"Well, I'll be!" Larry marvelled, "I'll never get through there though."

"We'll go and wait upstairs," Susan came to his rescue, no doubt as reluctant as I was to squeeze myself into that narrow entrance.

It was a horribly small space. We moved sideways, along the cavity behind the panelling between the bar and the office, eventually arriving at more planks going up. When we came out we were at the point in the crawling passage, upstairs, just where Martin had spotted something in the floor.

"I knew it, Alice!" he proudly proclaimed.

"Alright, Martin," I couldn't resist giving him another shove.

We had to thump on the entrance, of the fake wall around my brother's old room, until Larry and Susan let us out. When we surfaced, Sam looked around, amazed at all the art work.

"I had no idea this is what you get up to in here. You've kept that quiet."

"Well, we had no idea what you get up to down there," Larry replied.

"Did you ever go round this passage?" I could see where Susan was going with this question.

"No, I don't think I did, it's not a real one, like the others."

"That is a shame," she said, looking at me.

"I think my brother and I had worked out that you had been upstairs in The Inn; I probably recognised you, when you appeared in the bedroom. But we must have thought you made a habit of it. We left something for you, at the end of our secret passage."

"Go on, I can't imagine what," Sam looked confused at this revelation.

I pulled the motorbike key from my pocket and gave it to him. He looked at it for some time, turning it over in his hand.

"Where did you get this?"

"I'm afraid I don't know, but I think we left it for you, believing you would come for it. Sorry."

"You did me a favour, actually. There was a bad bunch of bikers; I met up with them on one of my little trips, further afield.

A few of them turned up here and started messing around, and I didn't want anything to do with them. Then lots of them came, and because I'd lost this key, I couldn't ride around with them and, more or less, hid until they eventually cleared out."

"I hate to ask, but did you ever take anything from The Inn?" I began to wonder if everyone had been wrong about him.

"No, but didn't I pay for what those bikers did. Of course, I was too scared to say it was them."

"Why did you tell me that Rachel was waiting for me at the butler's apartment; the time I got locked in The End House?"

"I didn't, I was thinking about telling her what was going on when I saw you in the little garden. I asked if you'd seen her and you must have followed me; that took some explaining, believe you me."

"I have no idea what's going on now," Martin, the detective, could hold his silence no more.

"It's a long story," Susan replied. "We'll fill you in on all the intricacies later."

"So, did the bikers know about the tunnels?" I wondered, "Could they have kept coming back, and have burgled the Inn the other night?" Although, they must be pretty ancient by now, I thought to myself.

"Well, they only used one way in and I blocked that off when they'd gone, but I do know who it was, I'm ashamed to say."

"Come on then!" Larry said, looking agitated.

"When the witches came the other day, I didn't know, but Agnes had decided she'd drum up a bit of trade; as I charge a small fee for entering the tunnels. She made some sort of invitation on Facebook and loads of idiots turned up."

"This is beginning to make sense; a bit," I thought over all the events at the gatehouse and The Inn. "Someone has been in the gatehouse, and moved our stuff around, and the bedroom furniture."

"I'm sorry, but can't say I'm surprised. Agnes seems to have been taking groups around down there for days. She knows our time's up, with the new development going ahead."

"I suppose her last little tour was on the night I was robbed?" Larry asked.

"It looks like it. I haven't seen her since, and that's unlike her. I'm a bit worried, to be honest."

"Does anyone else fancy a beer?" Larry said, heading out of my brother's old room, and we followed him downstairs.

I took Martin back to the gatehouse to collect Mrs Napper's tin; it was time to show Sam what was inside.

On the way back he asked "And just what exactly do you do when you're not going down holes in Norfolk?"

"Nothing that would interest you," it seemed too predictable in some ways, and I was still enjoying being Alice-returned too much to bring London-Alice to life.

Back inside The Inn, we found the others mulling over the possibility of how there might now be enough evidence to convince the brewery that the robbery was not Larry's fault.

"If you want, I could speak to them, and show them the tunnels, Larry?" Sam asked, seeming genuinely concerned for him.

"I must say, Sam, you're not at all what I expected."

"I could say the same, Alice," I wouldn't have thought he'd have any opinion of me as an adult. "Didn't you tell me to sod off, at The Circle, when I tried to introduce myself?"

"Oh God, I'd forgotten about that. I didn't know who you were and thought you were trying to intimidate me with the fox's head."

"What, with old Shifter here?" he said, patting the sad looking creature. "This is my old friend; he's nothing to be afraid of. He followed me around for years, as tame as your Bobby, and when his time came, I thought I'd keep him with me."

"Anyway, here is your aunt's secret hoard. Which reminds me; were you searching for this, on the first floor of the big house the other night? We could see a light in there; it seemed to be looking for something."

"No, but I can think of a few who might have been. We all knew Edith was on her way out."

"Come on Alice, open the blasted thing," Larry said, growing impatient.

I gently spread most of the items out on the bar, for everyone to see, and we let Sam examine each piece; silently waiting for his comments, as he looked at the photographs.

"Who really knows what sort of a marriage it was?" he sighed, holding the picture of Edith sitting on Shannon; with Evelyn standing by the horse's head. "I believe they were happy enough."

"Perhaps this is her way of saying that they were happy," Susan said, thoughtfully.

"They're smiling, and why else would she have kept this in the tin otherwise?" I suggested

"I think you could be right there," he said, carefully placing it down, and then picking up the other photograph. "I remember this as a painting; it used to hang in the morning room, downstairs. That room wasn't used for years. I have no idea where all the stuff went. The Nappers cleared the place out at some point."

"Who is the lady?" Martin asked. It was a black and white photograph of the painting; she had been set against a sky of fluffy clouds, and posed with a palette in one hand, and an artist's brush in the other.

"This is one of Edith's great-grandmothers, or further back. Unless I'm wrong, she was responsible for the painting of Cornelius Walker, on the stairway in The End House."

"That's amazing!" Martin exclaimed. "I haven't seen that, but do you think she painted the one on our stairs?"

"I would have thought they were by the same hand" I looked at Sam for confirmation of this.

"I would suspect so, as I don't suppose there were too many artists round here, back then."

I was surprised at how interested Sam was in the photographs. I expected him to look at the documents first.

"Now, Edith did tell me about this, I think she might even have shown it to me, when I was a boy," he said, eventually picking up and unfolding the map. It was a very old drawing of a cluster of small buildings in a hollow, with names that looked like surnames, next to each of them. At the centre of these was a stony mound, with what appeared to be an entrance.

"This is old Wythrum, before the Walkers, and the Nappers claimed it as their own. Cornelius Walker had the farmland, at the back of the place, and at some point, he took it into his head to drive these people out of here, and worse. They were just natural bodies, rubbing along with the land. He might be my ancestor, but I think he was wrong to do it."

"What do you make of this?" I asked, gesturing to the document with the wax seal, which stated the gambling debt.

He glanced over it, replying, "Oh, I knew about this alright. I don't suppose it cuts any ice though; it was all stitched up long ago."

"Did you ask Alice to do what she thought was best, with the contents of the tin?" Susan asked.

"I did," Sam calmly replied.

"Well, we took this to a solicitor, in Cromer today," she failed to add that we had shown it to more than one.

"Did you now?" he laughed.

"He seemed very interested in it, and would like to meet you," I wondered what his response would be.

"I don't see any harm in that," he didn't seem surprised; perhaps that's what he expected, or hoped for. I gave him the card with the telephone number; Sam said nothing more but placed it in a pocket, behind Shifter's head.

"There is something else," I said, producing the pendant from the tin. Having paid so much attention to the document, I hadn't really given this too much thought, but when I held it, I saw how grotesque it was. Behind the oval glass, a curl of hair nestled around the tiny painting of a man's eye; this was set in a black and gold surround. Turning it over, I noticed a yellow gem stone above the initials CW. "The label clearly states Walker and I'd imagine this is to show that it is not the property of the Napper family."

"I know it isn't!" Martin almost shouted. "Look at the photo of the artist in the painting; she's wearing it!"

"Now this is a turn up!" Sam appeared excited at this, despite how hideous it was. "At least there's something for my Agnes," he then looked quite sad. "I do wonder where she is."

"Don't you worry, boy," Larry said, confidently. "We'll find her".

Martin, Susan and I all glanced at each other, looking less so.

After this, we paraded about The Inn for the locking up, and then made our separate ways home. Back at the gatehouse, we shut the entrance to the tunnels and pushed the chest of drawers over it; just in case.

Chapter Twenty-two

It's all over now, Baby Blue

I had expected a quiet night, yet my dreams didn't allow me one. The last few weeks ran amok in them, casting symbols, windows and walls in my way. All those faces, which had now become familiar, dogged me as I dodged around the passages and buildings, still looking for something.

Awake and staring blankly at the ceiling, searching for anything of meaning through this bizarre montage, I was rudely brought into the new day.

"Who the hell is Arthur? You've been calling his name all night," Susan yawned, before hitting me with her pillow; which I noticed was mine.

"I have no idea. Anyway, never mind him for now; it's time to find Agnes."

"Oh no, I think that's going to be impossible; where on earth do we begin?"

"We'll go and get Martin, and then, who knows?"

As we opened the door to the car park, Martin was already heading our way. "Morning ladies," he waved to us. "Let the hunt for Agnes begin! Do you have any destinations in mind?"

"As it happens, I do, and just go along with anything I say."

I knew there weren't many places along Cart Lane large enough to be guest houses, so I imagined it would be easy to find

Mrs Cunningham's. We didn't have to walk far before I found the house I believed to be the most likely.

I may well have known it was Judith's old home, from my childhood memories. A weather-splintered, painted sign bore the name 'Phaeton Lodge'. The building, itself, was in some need of repair; the brickwork, which had been plastered and painted white at one time was now stained and crumbling; whilst many of the roof tiles hung perilously enough to deter all but the most determined of visitors.

Creeping to the front door, elbowing each other and stifling giggles, I tried to get my story straight before knocking. However, before I regained my composure, the man I had seen Judith with, at the open day to 'The End House' and on the ghost walk, opened it.

"I'm afraid we're not taking guests at present, you might like to try at the camp site."

"We're not looking for somewhere to stay; we're looking for Agnes. Is Judith at home?" This wasn't exactly what I meant to say; I had reached my point far too quickly, and could see he was taken aback by this.

"I represent bands in London, and am very interested in Agnes. I hoped that Martin here," Susan butted in, gesturing to him, "would be able to take some photographs of her for me, before I return."

"Oh well, I don't know? That's quite something else," he responded, flustered. "You'd better come in."

He took us to a large, very dated, sitting room; it must have been the one for the boarders, given the amount of arm chairs and side-tables, all turned in odd directions.

Eventually Judith appeared, looking cross and perplexed. "Alice, what are you doing here?"

"Didn't your husband," I threw this in to find out if she was married to him, "tell you why?"

"He did, but I don't believe it for one minute. Why are you looking for Agnes?"

"Because she needs to be found," I replied, unable to think of a better response.

"Very well, but she isn't here."

"Do you know any where she might be?" Martin asked, politely.

"Your guess is as good as mine, whatever it has to do with you," she replied, quite her usual self. "But if she's to be found, I'm coming with you."

We looked at each other in dismay as Judith took over; which I found irksome. She then abandoned us to the boring room, in order to make some phone calls; I couldn't imagine that she could be contacting anyone Sam wouldn't have already thought of. Looking about the place, although it must have been a nice house once, there was something deathly dull about it; no wonder she went off the rails. I almost forgave her for being so horrid to me.

Judith returned, looking even grumpier. "Well, that was a fat lot of good," she huffed. No doubt she had received frosty responses to her calls. "There is one place I can think of, where she might go. She's a bit of a romantic and often lurks around there. Come on then."

I had expected us to head back towards the village, but instead we continued down Cart Lane, in the direction of the campsite. I should have realised our destination; it was the abandoned Arts and Crafts house. This was thrilling; I had longed to have a peek inside but, until this point, had found no excuse for trespassing other than nostalgia and pure curiosity.

The house was beautiful and could almost have been three cottages joined together, as each section, with their sloping tiled roofs, appeared individual in design. An overgrown porch, shrouding a rounded door way at the front, announced the entrance. We retraced our footsteps from the night of the ghost walk, but this time continued up the overgrown path and made our way to the rear. There stood a tumbled down out-building, which I remembered as an aviary; the little door to this hung open, and its wire mesh was rusted and broken. I recalled warm summer's afternoons, orange squash, and the sound of children playing.

We made our way round to the far side of the house. Standing back, I counted fourteen windows, made up of thirty frames, and that this was just on one face of the building; I this found amazing. How sad it was that such a place could be left to fall into this lonely and unloved state. Blue plastic sheeting covered several of the slated projections, in a futile attempt at keeping the Norfolk rain out.

Martin tried the door at the rear, which wouldn't have been out of place in the times of Sir Lancelot, with its chequered dark wood and iron fittings. It opened willingly, and we entered a large room, which I instantly remembered as the family dining area; there was still a Welsh dresser built into the wall, and the floor was stained with the same mahogany coloured lacquer. Moving along, each of the many rooms offered something different to admire, but there was no time for this.

With no sign of Agnes downstairs we made our way up. I opened a door on the first landing and, finding that this revealed a bathroom, began to search for signs of recent use. A red toothbrush and a tube of toothpaste rested between the oxidised taps of the wash basin, and a flannel was neatly arranged on the rolled edge of the bath. We left and continued upwards.

After looking in at all the empty bedrooms, we eventually found ourselves at the door to one of the attic rooms. I shuddered, remembering Rachel's story of the artist's model. Susan lifted the iron latch and pushed the door open; beneath the window we could discern the shape of a body, in a green sleeping bag.

Judith ran towards this and knelt down, "Agnes, what are you doing here?" We froze, waiting for movement.

The room was littered with empty bottles, a few more sleeping bags, candles and a Ouija board.

"Oh shit!" Agnes shrieked, springing to life, and looked around like she had never seen the room before.

Martin rushed over, seeing that Judith's presence may have alarmed her, "Your dad's been looking for you, and we said we'd help. You're alright now."

"Just take your time," Susan added, attempting to soothe her.

"Everything's fine," I found myself saying. "You can come with us, and we'll take you to The Inn."

"She can come with me, thank you very much," Judith said, indignantly. "What have you been doing here?"

"Well, you should know, Mother," Agnes got up, straightening her dress out. "I've been showing people a proper haunting, but when it actually happened, they didn't like it and took off."

"Are you coming with me?" Judith asked.

"No, I don't think so."

"Alright then, that's your choice," and with this, she left. I found myself feeling sorry for her.

Making our way back to the village, Martin asked, "What did you mean by a proper haunting?"

"Oh, you know, orbs floating around, cold sensations, and the feeling that someone was sitting next to them. The usual stuff, but they worked themselves into a state and fell over each other on their way down the stairs. They wanted to experience it and then couldn't hack it."

"So, are you saying the place is really haunted?" Susan gasped.

"Of course it is, so is the whole village," I felt relieved to hear someone actually saying this for once. "There's not much else to make a living out of round here."

We took Agnes to The Inn, where she could have a bath and something to eat, while Martin went in search of Sam. It was unavoidable that Larry would question her about the robbery; this needed to be dealt with. I could see that he was biding his time, until she was comfortable enough to cope with it.

"So, Agnes, you must know I'm in a sticky situation. Did you take people down into the tunnels?"

"I did, and it got out of control, but this is the end of it for me, and my dad. I just wanted to make the most of it for him."

"But where does that leave me?" he replied, surprisingly calm.

"Don't worry, I'll tell the brewery all about it."

Just then, Martin appeared with Sam.

"There you are my luv, and what a time you've put me through." It was a touching reunion. Sam wasn't at all cross with her, and they soon shuffled off, back to the old farm, after thanking us.

"So much for the quiet village life," Martin laughed.

"I can certainly see what my parents said about this place. They're all a bit too close," saying this, I realised we had been neglecting Rachel and Don, and thought it was time for a visit to the camp site. We took Martin with us.

Chapter Twenty-three

I Put a Spell on You

There was no one in at the bungalow, but after walking around the site for a while, we found Rachel pruning bits of foliage and collecting them in a sack.

"It's Mrs Napper's funeral tomorrow, I'm going to make a wreath."

"I might be able to help you there, Rachel; I've got a bit of a knack with these things," Martin offered, looking pleased with himself.

"I see Don's been hard at work again," I said, admiring my former chalet. "It's a pity I'll be leaving so soon."

"Me too," Susan added, peering in at the windows, "I think I'll be staying here next time."

"You'd be more than welcome," Rachel added, seeming to be in a better mood with us. "It's strange to think of you both leaving; we'd sort of got used to having you around."

"What will you be going back to?" Martin asked. "It's hard to imagine what you both do, somewhere out there."

"I teach art at a secondary school," Susan replied.

"I should have guessed," he laughed. "And you, Alice? Come on, spill the beans now. Don't tell me, I bet you're a secret agent!"

"Very funny, Martin," I knew it was coming up to the time I would have to go back to being myself and had to admit what I had become. "I'm a Blue Badge London tourist guide."

“For heaven’s sake, Alice,” Rachel chimed in. “What on earth must you have made of my little ghost walk?”

“I thought it was rather good, actually; very professional,” I replied, with a wink.

“We’ll go and get this made up; you and Susan can sort out something to eat, if you don’t mind?”

We then held a sort of wake, for Mrs Napper and chatted about events so far, telling them of our progress. After dinner, Don placed the finished wreath on top of the juke box saying, “Let’s have some tunes for the lady.” He and Rachel jived about the room to Rock around the Clock, while we tried to keep up with them. Then, Screamin’ Jay Hawkins blared out, in tinny authenticity from the speakers as the three of us lolled around on the Chesterfield, whilst Don and Rachel performed a tango.

“Given what the document, in Mrs Napper’s tin, tells us about the gambling debt, it’s a funny coincidence that Evelyn and Edith married,” I observed.

They stopped in their tracks.

“Oh no, there’s nothing funny about it, nor was it a coincidence,” Don said.

“What do you mean?” Susan added, poking herself up the nostril with a cocktail umbrella.

“He had to marry a Walker; they knew the Napper’s time was up at The End House.” Rachel looked as though we should have worked this one out by now. “And if they’d had a child, things would have been different.”

"Have you always known this?" I asked, wondering if she hadn't always been troubled about the legal details of her properties.

"Oh no, only when I told Edith about your being here did she start reminiscing. I visited her every week, and she normally only talked about what had been on TV."

"Sam seemed to know about the document, but believed it would make no difference," I wished Susan had thought before saying this; Don must have been generous with that gin.

"Did he now?" Rachel said, suddenly looking very sober. "What else did he know about?"

"He'd seen the map we have of Old Wythrum before," I gave her a sharp elbow in the ribs as her words came out.

"Well, that explains a few things, so it does," Don seemed to know all about both documents.

"Hello, I'm getting very lost here," Martin exclaimed, sitting up as straight as he could.

"Until the other day, I thought Gail wasn't *old village*, but after quizzing her I realised that she's about as old as it gets. Her family were from here. Something else I never knew was that Samuel and Gail are married," Rachel appeared animated by her own words.

"And, what difference does that make?" I asked, getting a bit lost myself.

"He's hedging his bets. She's chased him around for a divorce for years. He's not sure who it all belongs to and doesn't want to lose out."

"Surely, she can just get a divorce?" Susan thumped her glass angrily down on the table. "I bloody well did!"

"Perhaps she doesn't really want one," Martin grinned, knowingly. "Have you got that photo, Alice?"

I took everything out of my pockets and found the photograph.

"What do you make of that, Rachel?" he asked, still grinning.

"It's Gail and Sam, having an argument," she shrugged.

"Yes, it is, but I remembered what I saw; after taking this," Martin said, looking impressed with himself.

"Stop skirting around, and spit it out," I demanded.

"They had a good old snog!" he rocked back against the creaking leather, satisfied with his disclosure and smirked into his glass, as we all looked about, shocked at the idea of this.

"I don't think I can take any more revelations today. It's time to go; we've got the funeral tomorrow," I began to feel afraid that anything I had previously done might surface in this atmosphere.

"You're coming then?" Rachel said looking pleased. "I hoped you would."

Back at the gatehouse, as usual, I didn't have the good night's sleep I was anticipating. This time it wasn't due to dreams, or lights from The End House; it was from a horribly, familiar sensation that we weren't alone in the room. The Night Walker had been disturbed. I imagined all the ghosts of the village paying their visits to those seeking slumber, on the eve of Mrs Napper's funeral. I was very glad that the hideous pendant was now in the possession of Samuel Walker, and hoped that he would be able to deal with the owner of that hair, should he venture his way

Chapter Twenty-four
The Days of Pearly Spencer

By the time we arrived at the church next to The End House, accompanied by Martin and Larry, most of the funeral party were assembled and awaiting the arrival of the hearse. Gail was chatting with Rachel and Don; I would have enjoyed hearing that conversation. Judith, her husband, and mother stood in silence amongst the graves, whilst Sam and Agnes spoke to the vicar. There were a few others there, who I didn't recognise, and wondered if they were Nappers, Walkers or simply locals, come to pay their respects.

Sam and Don were the lead pallbearers, carrying the coffin, decked out with Rachel's wreath, and a spray of wild flowers. I assumed the other men were from the undertaker's company, as they were the only ones in formal funeral dress.

A recording of Joseph Haydn's, La chasse was played, during the procession into the church; no doubt, as a reference to Edith's hunting days. I remembered reading somewhere that Haydn wanted to suggest that the fox got away.

From our pew, near the back, I glanced at Judith, seated piously towards the front, and remembered her shutting me in the chapel at school; with the other elderly lady in her coffin.

A simple mass was performed by the vicar, after which he called upon the nephew of Mrs Napper, Samuel Walker, to come forward and give a reading. I expected this to be from the Bible, but Sam produced a sheet of paper and began to recite something else entirely.

"From this cave and up, they drove them out. On this land and down, they bricked them in. Dig them up and bring them round, Cornelius Walker's gone to ground," he growled. As the vicar looked on with increasing horror, I wondered how Sam had got on with the hairy pendant during the previous evening, and if this hadn't had some affect on his behaviour.

After an uncomfortable pause, the sound of a guitar trembled over the congregation, and Agnes began to sing Mona Lisa, the Nat King Cole song, whilst Sam stood with one hand on Edith's coffin; even from the back, I could see his shoulders juddering in grief.

There was the unmistakable creak of wood, as the coffin was lifted from its catafalque, and I then watched Edith carried by, back down the aisle. At this point, I caught sight of two people, failing to be inconspicuous; in the alcove by door. I recognised the outline of the young woman, by the curl of her fringe, and tailored jacket; it was the solicitor from Gilmont, Gilmont and Associates. She was with an older man, whom I assumed to be her father.

We made our slow walk, out into the graveyard, and gathered around the opened gate of 'The End House' vault; I noticed Sam becoming agitated.

"You'd better be waiting for her," he shouted down into the darkness. "You'd best be taking care of her, or I'll be after you, Napper!" Agnes took his arm and led him to one side.

After "We have entrusted our sister", the vicar's words then became a blur, as I looked around at those gathered. Sam and

Agnes held hands as they scattered petals onto the coffin, followed by Rachel, Don and Gail.

The funeral director and his men then carried her down the steps, and into the darkness of the vault. I wished my old friend farewell, more tearfully than I had anticipated.

The party then made their way to The Inn, where food had been prepared, and those gathered stood about remembering what they knew, but had forgotten, about the life of Edith, between nibbles and sips.

I then noticed that some printed cards had been placed on each table; I picked one up and read, 'By the request of Edith Napper, the presentation of her last will and testament is to take place in the ballroom of The End House, at 3p.m. today.

I could almost hear the sound of buzzard's wings flapping at this, and as it was only mid-day this left plenty of time for feathers to be ruffled before the appointed hour. I wondered if she hadn't done this on purpose.

"What did you make of Sam's speech," Susan whispered to me from behind a cheese straw?"

"It would seem he knows a lot more about the tunnels than he's let on."

"Do you really think there are bodies down there?" she added, with a shiver.

"It wouldn't surprise me; nothing would to be honest."

A pair of hands then grabbed me by the shoulders, and I almost collapsed. "I can guess what you're talking about," Martin breathed in my ear.

"For goodness sake, Martin," I spluttered, giving him a small kick to the ankle. "I wish you wouldn't do that."

"I think it's going to get a lot scarier than that before tomorrow," he mouthed, nodding towards the others.

Larry appeared next to us, with a tray of our usual tipples. "Well, that was a turn up; I think I'll need a bit of assistance in getting off tonight, knowing what's down there."

"You're not the only one," I said, gladly taking my glass. "No wonder there are all those marks, warding off witches, about the place. They must have been scared out of their wits."

"Now, there's something else very strange," Susan said, leading us with her eyes to the bar, where Rachel, Don, Gail and Sam all appeared to be chatting happily.

"In all my years here, I've never seen that before," Larry marvelled at the situation, sipping his pint. "No, I've never seen Rachel, or Don, exchange as much as one word with Sam."

"Perhaps they've realised that they might need him on their side; who knows what's in that will?" I suggested.

Suddenly, feeling a bit peckish, I headed over to the food, where I met Agnes, staring blankly at a pile of sandwiches. I asked her if she was feeling ok.

"I'm fine, thanks again for the other day. I'm sorry that I've caused so much trouble round here," she smiled, choosing an egg and cress but just holding it above the paper plate, seemingly unable to raise it to her lips.

"Why don't we sit down? You could probably do with a rest," she certainly didn't look alright.

As we did so, I noticed Judith hovering nearby, observing us.

Lifting my hand, I wiggled my fingers at her, in an embarrassingly feeble attempt at a friendly gesture. Spotting this,

Agnes released a slow sigh, before beckoning her over, "Would you like to join us, Mother?"

"Thank you, Agnes," she said, taking the seat next to mine. "I'm sorry about yesterday, both of you. Alice, I know you were just trying to help; but you did give me a terrible shock, Agnes."

"I know," she replied, lifting the lid of the sandwich and examining its contents. "It all seemed like a good idea at the time, but I know it was a stupid thing to do."

"Perhaps you should see if you can help Rachel out, with her ghost tours?" I suggested. "I'm sure you would be an excellent double act."

"What a good idea, Alice," Judith agreed, to my surprise. "We should speak to her about it, don't you think, Agnes?"

"Maybe, but we'll leave that for another day," she replied, looking a tad more cheerful at this suggestion.

Mother Cunningham came over to join us. "Agnes, dear," she said, stooping down and giving her a peck on the cheek, before falling into a chair.

"Mrs Cunningham, I'm sure we'd all love to hear any recollections you have of dear Mrs Napper?" I asked, changing the subject, unsure of the response this would receive.

"Edith was a lovely woman, very brave, and clever," Mrs Cunningham spoke with her eyes looked inwards, at her memories. "She took you in, Judith, the little horror that you were then, and let you sleep on a camp bed in her room; she told me you were too scared to stay in any of the other bedrooms."

"I didn't know she told you about it?" Judith blushed.

"Of course she did, she was too well mannered not to. And she sent you money, to help you out in London; after you left. She told me not to worry, and that she would keep in touch with you; when you wouldn't with me. There I was, left with Agnes here, you lovely girl; while you, Judith, went around reading cards," she said, smiling again at her granddaughter.

"You stayed in The End House, with Mrs Napper? I asked, having the feeling that Larry may have told me this before. "Lucky you, I would have loved to stay there with her."

"Yes, it was quite an experience. She had all sorts of rituals I had to follow, mostly about securing the place for the night, but some of them involved lighting candles and chanting the names of past residents."

"No wonder you didn't fancy staying alone, in any of the other rooms!" I hadn't realised that Mrs Napper had been prey to such superstitions. "Was she always alone there? I seem to remember her friend staying there."

"I can answer that," Mother Cunningham spoke. "It wasn't unusual for the time, I suppose; her old friend, Iris, lived with the farmer, at the back there. They weren't married, you know, but these things happened after the war." She continued, "Every morning Iris would go and get her up, sorting her out for the day, and then she would go back in the evening and help her to bed. Years later Rachel would also go in and give her a hand, letting herself in and out."

"I have just remembered something that might put your mind at rest about me." I rooted around in my pocket and took out the little drawing I had found in the shoe box, and the one drawn by Martin. "Do you remember the picture I drew?"

"Oh yes, I do, you little creature," she was transported back to her usual mood.

"Take a look at these," I offered, presenting her with both drawings. "I showed Martin, who lives here at The Inn, this drawing I did as a child, and this was his re-creation of it. It's Doctor Who, Mrs Cunningham, there was no dagger, no stabbing; 'the dagger' was just a tool Doctor Who used. I had no idea that Mr Napper was stabbed."

"If you say so, Alice," she didn't look convinced. "It's a bit of a coincidence though."

"There are plenty of those around here," I said, in my defence.

Despite this hiccup, the funeral breakfast was not the bun fight I'd been anticipating; everyone was getting on better than ever before. I wondered if old Edith hadn't been casting a spell or two.

"Where's your husband, Judith?" I asked, noticing he wasn't in the bar. "I haven't really had the chance to meet him properly."

"He's gone back to take Mother's little dog out." The word 'dog' bothered me. I glanced over at the door and imagined Bobby, wagging his black tail; asking to go out into the beer garden. Then I remembered the picture my brother had sent me, of the Great Dane, and saw my little self being knocked into the fireplace, again, by the huge, overenthusiastic creature; which had also wreaked havoc here, on the day of the hot pants competition.

Sam Walker then came over.

"Ladies, do you think it would be fitting for us to take a stroll about the place, before the reading of the will? I believe we would all benefit from the air." I was speechless at this. "Mother Cunningham," he said, offering his arm to her.

"Thank you, Mr Walker," she rose, leaning against him. "That sounds like a very good idea."

I wondered, what on earth was going on round here? These people, normally without a good word to say about each other, seemed to have been thrown back to Georgian manners.

By now, only the ten of us remained; there had been no mystery Walkers or Nappers. The others, it appeared, had just been locals, or old friends of Edith's. Gilmont and Gilmont hadn't shown their faces at the Inn, but I could feel them lurking around close by; awaiting the moment when they would deliver the bequests.

Sam proceeded to take us on a tour, giving a commentary, as though we were completely new to the place.

"Now, these were the stables of The End House which Edith's husband developed into The Inn as we know it, although there had long been a small ale house at the front of the stables. Even until the early sixties, the back part there, now the cellar, still housed horses, including Edith's Shannon. She could see her when she wanted, from the windows on that side," he said gesturing to the big house. "She loved that mare; she was a present from Evelyn on her fortieth birthday."

"Was that before the accident?" Susan asked.

"No, it was after. If you noticed, in the photograph, Edith was riding on the off-side, whereas most ladies rode to the near. They had a special saddle made for her, as her injury was to the right side."

"What do you know about the accident?" this had been on my list, I remembered.

"Alice, you must recall Alf, the cellar man, when you lived here?"

"I do, he was a particular friend of mine. We have a photo, from the library, of his father as a beater at one of the shoots."

"Yes, that's right. Well, he always maintained that one of the gentlemen dropped his gun but that there was the sound of two shots, when Edith fell. Who will ever really know what happened? It was never clear."

"I believe it was some Napper or other, wanting to kill her off, so there were no children for her to pass the place onto," Mother Cunningham said, angrily.

"But, surely, there was Sam's family, waiting in the wings; if the return of the place to the Walkers is to be believed?" Susan asked.

"And look at what happened to his parents," she said, clinging more fiercely to his arm.

"My parents were keen sailors; we used to go out all the time, in their little boat. One Sunday, for no reason, we started sinking somewhere off Cromer. I had a life jacket on, but they never wore them. The life boat picked me up; they were never found. Edith and Evelyn brought me up after that."

"How awful, I'm sorry to hear that Sam," I shuddered; there did seem to be a curse on the Walker family, or something else, even more sinister, at play.

"After that, I wasn't allowed anywhere on my own for years. Edith was always on the look out. In the end I rebelled."

"What about Evelyn's death, at The Inn? I understand he was stabbed, and that his assailant was never discovered." This was also a mystery still to be solved.

"That's true, but he had ruined enough people round here for no one to point the finger, rampaging around with the hunt, like he owned the whole district; without a care in the world."

"And the gatehouse, Sam, how was that used when you were a boy?" Susan asked.

"A sort of head grounds man lived there, with his wife. He was shifty bugger; it was through following him that I discovered the tunnels. There was still smuggling going on then, I think he was in cahoots with Evelyn on this, but I never saw him down there."

"I hope you don't mind my asking, but someone's got to," Martin asked, eagerly. "What was that speech you made; did you compose it for the service?"

"I wondered when that would come up; I'm surprised no one has mentioned it before," he grinned, and looked slowly at all gathered around him. "Those are the words the Witches of Waltham end each of their vigils with, in the lower circle."

"What part do you play, in these gatherings, Sam?" Larry asked, looking very uncomfortable, no doubt imagining all this going on beneath him for years.

"I am the keeper of the passages, I stand by, and guard them; with my trusty Shifter," he gestured to the fox.

"It's almost three o'clock," Susan said, sounding alarmed at the arrival of the appointed hour.

"Do you mind if I lead?" I asked Sam, wanting, for one last time, to experience my walk through the old door, and up the staircase; as if alone again.

"Not at all," he answered, stepping to one side.

I tried to hear the crunch of gravel, beneath my little shoes; imagining a day when I was six-years old, picturing Mrs Napper, waiting for me with the chocolate gingers, watering can and gramophone.

My hand glided, once more, along that familiar banister, as we made our way to the first floor. The door to the grand room was open; we then saw that a long table and chairs had been brought up for the event.

The Gilmonts were waiting for us, seated at the top of this, with their backs to the windows; there was a collection of tea chests, and other boxes, below these. Taking our seats in silence, we studied each other, the room and the Gilmonts.

"Good afternoon, I am Algernon Gilmont, of Gilmont, Gilmont and Associates," the elderly gentleman began. His Edwardian styled dark suit, round-collared white shirt and dotted tie seemed fitting for the occasion; as did the gold pocket watch, which he opened, pronouncing that it was now three of the clock. "It is my duty now to read to you the last will and testament of Edith Napper, formerly Edith Walker; following the instructions of the deceased lady." The click of the closing watch case was audible.

He continued with the revoking of all former wills, before stating that Rachel Moore was the appointed executor.

"I have been instructed to deliver the minor bequests first. 'To Judith Cunningham, I leave the contents of the tea chest bearing your name'. There is a list here, but it may be more gratifying to discover the items at your own perusal. An identical bequest is made to Rachel Moore; yours is the large travelling trunk," he glanced around the table, seeking acknowledgement from them both.

"Somewhat unusually, there has been a more recent bequest, made in the form of a letter. This has been witnessed by Aisling Dewer; whom I understand to be the superintendent of The Ashby Nursing Home. He peered over his round, tortoiseshell spectacles, "To Alice Cartwright; I bequeath my side saddle, riding habit, and other items associated with my beloved Shannon. These are in the large wooden crate with the stable plate bearing, not surprisingly, the name Shannon.'"

I was very touched, but had no idea what I would do with these treasured items.

He continued, "Before distributing the gifts below, I instruct my executor to pay all my debts, funeral and testamentary expenses, and all government duties that may be payable, in the event of my death. I give, Agnes Cunningham, provided she survives me by thirty days, any money I possess. I give, providing he survives me by thirty days, Samuel Walker, any property I possess." Keeping his head lowered, he stated "The monies left to Agnes amount to the sum of twelve thousand, three hundred and seventy-two pounds, in my estimation. However, I'm afraid; there is no property for you, Mr Walker."

"Quite the contrary, I believe," a voice came from the door way; Adrian Hodges entered the room. He strolled, nonchalantly, towards the Gilmonts, and then placed, what I imagined to be, a copy of the photocopied document on the table before them. "This throws a different light onto these proceedings. The proposed development of The End House must be brought to a halt, until the implications of this recently discovered document are thoroughly explored."

We all clapped at this, and Sam called out, "Well done girls!"

The Gilmonts left, closely followed by a satisfied looking Adrian Hodges, and we then began to explore our various boxes. Rachel and Judith produced a splendid array of dresses, silk undergarments, porcelain figurines and jewellery. I was amazed to see, on opening my crate, that the first item was the bubble wrapped portrait of Edith and Shannon. Perhaps, I thought, this was meant to remind me of where she kept her little tin; had I not already recalled this. Enclosed between the flaps of the saddle, there was a soft pile, wrapped in brown paper. I undid this and revealed her riding costume; the long, black boots stood upright at opposite ends of the crate.

I took the boots and costume into Edith's old room and, thinking of her, dressed in what was, most likely, her favourite outfit. It was a little stiff and musty smelling, but so was I. Drawing down the fine black net, from the bowler hat, over my chin, I walked back towards the others; with the boots resounding in a fabulous echo on the old floor, and along the corridor.

"Jesus Christ!" Sam exclaimed. "Edith's back."

I made a pantomime sweep at my thigh with the hunting whip, and everyone fell about in amusement.

"Someone get the lady a horse, and we could scare the village right up!" Larry guffawed. "Come on everybody; let's take her back to The Inn."

Again, leading the procession, we made our way down the stairs. I paused at the painting of Cornelius Walker. "Here he is, Martin," and we all gathered round, to inspect the old rascal.

Rachel took out her bunch of keys, and locked The End House up for the night. I wondered what Edith, and any other remaining spirits, had made of our visit there. Feeling the excitement she once must have enjoyed, I climbed down the stone steps, dressed for the hunt.

Martin couldn't resist insisting that I pulled down the veil again, and enter The Inn alone.

Whilst they lurked around, beneath the porch, I lifted the old latch and walked, as slowly as I could, towards the bar; pausing briefly, to admire myself in the yellowed mirror which hung over the fireplace. As I did this, a hush spread over the customers and then, pulling up the net, I revealed my face to the barman; ordering a pint of his best ale.

"Don't you ever tell me that I've lost the atmosphere of The Inn again, you sorry suppers!" Larry's voice rang out behind me. "Let's all have a drink, to Edith Napper, you miserable old bunch; on the house. Now you're smiling!"

Susan and I went behind the bar, one last time, to help serve up this tribute to Edith.

Generous, as always, Larry kept the drinks flowing, and everyone enjoyed the evening. Agnes provided the entertainment, singing a few bawdy music hall numbers. I winced, when I noticed the pendant swinging about her chest; wondering at the wisdom of her wearing this but kept my thoughts to myself.

"We're off now, Alice," Judith Cunningham said, hugging me. "I am glad you came back."

"And I'm off tomorrow, so I probably won't see you again," I smiled, amazed at this show of affection.

"You know where we are, so don't be a stranger," and she left, with Mother Cunningham; both of them, giving me a cheery wave.

My last evening at The Inn petered out with the ring of the bell for last orders, and the gradual exiting of the customers, some of whom couldn't resist a closer inspection of my costume; trying on the hat, and lifting my skirts to see what was underneath.

"Here's our final round together," Larry said, when there was only him, Martin, Susan and I left. We all stared quietly into our glasses. "It's been interesting; I'll say that."

Before the locking up ceremony, we made a last tour of my old home. I saw my little self everywhere; on the stairs; in the sitting room, crunching on endless pickled onions, and up in my bedroom. I glimpsed myself, trying to shut out the sounds of the ghosts, with brief images of all my family who had visited, and the much loved Bobby; always following us. It was quite emotional, knowing that I was returning to the loss of another home I felt so dear.

"So, this is it," Martin said, giving me a gentle shove.

"We'll come and say goodbye tomorrow," Susan mumbled, emotionally, giving him a big kiss on the lips, and then Larry, too. "This has been the best holiday ever."

I pulled the veil down and walked, with the determination of Edith, to the night awaiting us at the gatehouse.

We didn't bolt the bedroom door or pull the drawers over the entrance to the tunnel. Instead, we lit a candle, and invited all the spirits in; hoping for one final revelation.

Chapter Twenty-five
The Sound of Silence

There was no storm, and no torrential rain; the night was as hushed as the vault where Edith now rested. However, whether it was the result of Edith's costume, or the beer; in my dreams I galloped around the countryside, jumping perilous ditches and dodging other riders, to the sound of the horn and hounds, and the relentless breathing of the grey mare beneath me. I charged, on and on.

Woken by the sound of Susan's snoring and snuffling about, and noticing, again, that she somehow had possession of my pillow, I let my mind climb down the hidden ladder beneath the bedroom, and wandered along those dark tunnels; too scared to actually take another solo excursion into the labyrinth beneath Wythrum.

Feeling that sleep would never return, and with the knowledge that this was my last night, I dressed as silently as I could. I then began to worry about the painting, and riding costume; I would have to get them sent on somehow. Looking out of the window, at the big house, I became overwhelmed with sadness, and sat on the floor, over the secret entrance. It dawned on me that I might have nowhere to take these precious items to; I'd come back to a home that I had lost, at a time when I was about to be kicked out of my current one. As I pinched my hand, in a vain attempt to resist the flow of tears that were surfacing, I heard a voice.

"What the hell are you doing?" Susan asked, lifting her head, from my pillow.

"Getting ready to go," I replied, wondering how I must have felt all those years ago, on the night that I knew I was leaving here, for London, the next day.

We were interrupted by the sound of my mobile, which, at some point, I must have switched to vibrate again; it throbbed and span on the floor, next to the bed. Terrified, I grabbed at it, and answered.

"Hello," I whispered, not knowing why, but it seemed appropriate for receiving a call in the middle of the night.

"It's me, Larry," he was also whispering. "We can hear the stones, on the outside walls of The Inn being scraped; whatever it is has come back."

"Give us a few minutes and we'll be over," I stumbled about, looking for my boots. "Get dressed, Susan! Something's happening at The Inn." Be careful what you wish for; I thought to myself.

Walking across the lawn in the darkness, just about making out the familiar silhouette of Martin's upturned backside, I also spotted Larry's outline; he seemed to be feeling the walls.

"Bloody hell", Susan exclaimed, as we saw the amount of flint stones on the floor around The Inn.

Abandoning the pile he had collected, Martin arose, saying "Come on, let's go and get Sam."

I popped the smallest piece of flint I could find into my pocket, before we all hurtled round to the old farm and Larry banged, breathless, on the door. There was no sign of life; Susan peered through the windows, as I saw a dim light appear upstairs.

"Who's that?" Sam's voice called out, amid the thump of his footsteps. The door then opened, and despite wearing only his underpants, Shifter still swung from his side.

"I might have known; come in you lot," he said, as we followed into the kitchen, where he proceeded to rifle around the clotheshorse; before putting on a t-shirt and jeans. "Now, where did I leave my boots?"

"They are returned," Agnes whispered, as she emerged in her father's tracks, and I didn't think she meant his boots. Even the most sceptical would have had to admit that she appeared enchanted; her eyes swam around in the back of her head, while her arms felt their way forward.

"Good grief, Agnes," Larry called out. "Are you alright, girl?"

"Don't make a fuss, she's fine. What's going on now?" Sam asked.

"The stones have been coming off the walls at The Inn; just like they used to," Martin spoke, with the authority of someone who knew what was going on, when none of us actually had a clue.

"We won't find anything up here," Sam answered. "We must go down."

He took us to the side of the first outbuilding, where I now imagined that Martin had taken the photograph of him crouching. What had looked like a pile of stones now appeared to be a more significant structure.

"This was the ice house, to The End House," Sam said, lifting stone slabs away. "I had to close it off, after the bikers came, but opened it up when I had no easy way under the house.

Beneath the slabs there was a small drop into a narrow earthy pit. To our amazement, he then turned on a string of lights, illuminating a tunnel. This was different to the other passages; the walls appeared to be made of very ancient stone. "Wait here, moment," and we stood about, nervously, after he had pushed back past us; soon reappearing, armed with a shovel and pick axe. I didn't like the way things were going, nor did the others if the look on their faces was anything to go by.

With Sam leading, we eventually came to the end of this tunnel; coming to a halt at the mouth of an alcove. From this he produced caged lanterns and lit their enclosed candles with the broad flame of a petrol-fuelled lighter; passing them to each of us.

"I don't like this, old boy," Larry whispered to Sam.

"Has to be done, my friend," he spoke, without looking at any of us.

After travelling a short distance, we emerged into the circular space. Sam then lit the candles around the pentagram. "You all sit down here, think your best thoughts, and I'll be back in a jiffy," with this, he entered the mouth of the cave.

We sat in silence, with Martin apparently fighting the urge to laugh his head off, as grunts and blasphemous utterances issued from the stony arch that Sam had disappeared into; amid sounds of digging and scraping.

"Nearly there," he called out.

"Nearly where, I'd bloody like to know," Larry muttered.

With the arrival of an unexpected draught, all the candles were blown out; apart from those in the glass cages.

"I don't like this!" Susan called out, springing in front of Martin. "If you think it's so funny, you can be first for whatever happens next."

"Nothing's going to happen," he said, putting an arm around her.

"Here we are," Sam spoke softly; calmly emerging from the cave. It took a moment for my eyes to focus on the pile he was carrying.

"Jesus Christ," Larry called out, having seen what I thought I had.

Just then, there was a loud scream behind me. We jumped up, knocking the lanterns over, and began running, blindly, for the tunnel mouths.

"Don't panic," a familiar voice rang out. I turned and saw that it was Don, with Rachel and Gail poised, awkwardly, behind him.

"For goodness sake, you nearly scared me to death. How did you get in here?" Susan roared.

"You told us about the entrance in the gatehouse, Susan," apparently, I wasn't the only blabber mouth. "We couldn't sleep, and came over for a walk, when we saw you all going off somewhere. I thought it would be a good time to have a look down here. Gail is spending the night with us." Don explained, holding his hands out in a show of innocence.

"It was too tempting not to see what's down here," Rachel added.

"What have you done, Sam?" Gail shouted, in horror, gripping her hair.

"It's time they sorted it out for themselves," he said, kneeling in the centre of the pentagram, spreading out the collection of skulls and bones that he bore in his arms.

"Isn't this illegal, to say the least?" Martin asked. "Surely, we should tell the police what you have discovered, and leave them where they are for now?"

"Nobody, except the witches, and myself have been interested in the whereabouts of these poor souls for two hundred odd years. Don't tell me the police would know what to do with them."

Although this was said without anger, it was clear that, despite his years, it would not have been a good idea to interfere with his plans; what ever they were.

From the shadows Agnes then began to warble a beautiful folk song, about a young man falling in love with a shepherdess, who went on to refuse him.

"You know it's time, Gail," Sam took off his t-shirt and began to wrap the bones in it. "Cornelius Walker took a fancy to a local girl, the daughter of the village chief, as such, but when this didn't go his way he took his anger out on the whole lot of them. Gail is her descendent."

Holding the gruesome find before him, Sam led us down the tunnel that would take us to the gatehouse, but then turned into one that branched off from this.

"You go and tell him how it is," he said to the bundle, as he placed it on the floor, before lifting several planks and then pulling a heavy wooden door towards himself. From the light of his lantern we then saw coffins, ancient and more recent, laid out in rows on the stone tiled floor; it was the crypt where Edith's body had been placed earlier that day. Waiting at the entrance, we watched, as Sam swung his light over the oldest of these, until he fixed it on one; almost collapsed in on it self. Reading the plaque on the lid aloud, Sam spat the words "Cornelius Walker, Founding Father of Wythrum, brought to rest, 1825," he then stamped his foot on this, and raged, "Wake up you murderous swine; you've got visitors," before laying his t-shirt, and its contents, on the lid.

We lurked around in speechless horror, until Sam came out and closed the door behind him, slotting the planks back into place. "That should do it," he spoke quietly, before leading us back, and out of the entrance by the farm.

Standing about, with the violet murk of an early summer's night playing around us, Gail took Sam's hand and announced, "I am staying here; with my husband." We left them, and Agnes, beginning our slow walk back round to The Inn; pausing below the windows to my old bedroom.

"They didn't mention you when I took on the job of running The Inn," Larry called up at the image in the glass.

"I know exactly what you mean," I said, taking his arm.

We watched as Rachel and Don disappeared down Cart Lane, before Larry opened the door from the garden to The Inn.

"What the hell?" he cried out, breaking away from me, and running towards the bar.

Following behind him, we could see beer and lager gushing from the taps. This couldn't have been going on for long, as there was only a small puddle on the floor, and, unless I imagined it, I could swear that I saw the slab behind the fire place closing, but decided to keep this to myself.

“How am I going to explain this one to the brewery?” he asked, as we all flipped the taps off.

“I wouldn’t worry too much,” Susan said, with a knowing grin “You’ve got a haunted inn; a valuable commodity!”

“Would you mind if, for old time’s sake, I spend what’s left of my last night here in my old bedroom?” I asked, suddenly felling very tired, but didn’t wait for a response, and made my way up the stairs; passing the painting of my old demon.

Without turning on the light, I kicked off my boots and sank down on the single bed, letting my mind glance over the list of things I had wished to uncover, during my unexpected visit. Once satisfied, I drifted off into a pleasant sleep.

Chapter Twenty-six
I Wanna Be Your Dog

"Rise and shine!" Larry said, cheerfully patting me on the shoulder, as I awoke, to him, Martin and Susan standing by the bed. "We've got something ready for you downstairs."

When they had left, allowing me to sort myself out, I put on my boots meaning to join them, but instead found myself stroking the old mantle piece and taking one last look at my former bedroom, in the realisation that I had not discovered everything. I then headed to the bathroom, having not even glanced in there during our previous visits upstairs. On examining my face in the mirror, which wasn't an appetising sight, I closed my eyes and tried to remember the important thing that I had somehow forgotten. On opening them, I caught a reflection of my little self, looking inconsolable and was, yet again, wracked with a feeling of guilt.

I then made my way past The Night Walker in the painting, stopping briefly to say 'Boo!' to him, and climbed slowly down the stairs; imagining that I carried a small blue weekend case in one hand, with the brown satchel hung over my shoulder; just as I would have done, on that final morning at The Inn.

On a table, at the far end of the garden, my friends had laid out a parting breakfast, which included a bowl of pickled onions; from where I could enjoy the best view of The Inn, gatehouse and The End House. I didn't say or eat much, instead I let distant and recent events mingle in my mind's eye.

After this, Susan and I collected our belongings, accompanied by Martin and Larry; who had promised to look after my treasures from Mrs Napper, until I could provide them with a home. Then, taking a final look in the gatehouse bedroom, I lifted the entrance to the tunnel, shuddering at the thought that all of this had been beneath my little self, all those years ago, when I slept at The Inn.

Feeling around for a tissue in my pocket, I found the list I had made, with the wifi address on the back and wished for a connection with something:

1. Who shot Mrs Napper and why?
2. What did I used to keep in my pocket; and in our collection (where ever that went)?
3. What were the late night events at The Inn?
4. What happened at the Western Day?
5. Who was the other man with a motor bike?
6. What did I draw that shocked people?

I felt satisfied that all of these, at least, had been answered, as best as they could be. However, I was glad that some things might always remain a mystery and stoked the stone in my pocket.

"And what do we have here?" Martin asked, pretending to take a peep at the piece of paper.

"You can have this, as a souvenir," I said, handing it to him. "If some of it doesn't make sense, there are a few people you could ask."

"Yes, I can ask some of my new friends," he replied, with the customary wink.

Then, the four of us made our way to the train station, where Rachel, Don, Sam, Agnes and Gail were already assembled to bid us farewell.

Gail handed Susan a large, brown paper bag. "I saw you looking at this, and thought it might be useful one day," she said, smiling, with an impish look in her eye.

"A ouijja board!" Susan exclaimed, looking in the bag, unable to hide her alarm amid the gratitude she felt. "Thanks Gail, I don't know what to say."

"This is for you, Alice," Sam said, quietly to me, almost embarrassed. "It's not a very good likeness," glancing at Martin, as he put a small framed photo of himself and Shifter, when he was alive, in my hand.

"I will treasure this; it will remind me of you, and not to be so suspicious in future!" I gave my former demon a hug, avoiding the fox, before putting the photo in my pocket; for evidence.

After our goodbyes, and as Wythrum disappeared into the distance, the one thing I wanted to resolve sprang again into my mind. I took out my mobile and searched for the number.

"Hello, it's me."

"Hello, you," my dad answered.

"I'm on the train for London, just leaving the village. Can I ask you a question?"

"Yes, but I can guarantee that you won't like the answer," he replied, clearly knowing what was coming.

"Who died before we left The Inn?" I rattled off.

"Arthur," he replied, quietly.

There was a silence, but from me this time, as I remembered being told that I had called out this name when hypnotised, and in my sleep.

"Who was Arthur?" I asked, feeling my heart plummet at my own words.

"Arthur was Rachel's Great Dane. You let him out of the courtyard, during the western day, when you went looking for her. He was never seen again, and presumed dead."

I thought for a moment. "Now hold on, surely Sam Walker let him out."

"No, he always used the turnstile when Arthur was in the yard; like everyone else. When he realised she wasn't there and left, the gate was open; which should have told him that someone had followed him into the house. I did have a word, or two, with him about this, and I'm sure you've been reminded of this by now. You always liked to open the gate because it made the bell ring. I did warn you not to go snooping around; even then."

I pictured the image of the dog my brother had sent, all the bolts and latches that I'd enjoyed the feel of, and the gate to the courtyard, which had fascinated me. I then remembered Arthur, pushing me out of the way, to the clattering of the bell, and watching helplessly as he ran into the drive. Seeing my guilty, tear-stained, little self once more, I finally understood their deception.

Parents don't always tell their children everything; and probably for good reason.

The End

(For the time being)

13051051R00136

Printed in Great Britain
by Amazon